PENGUIN BOOKS

1794

THE ORDEAL OF GILBERT PINFOLD
TACTICAL EXERCISE
LOVE AMONG THE RUINS

EVELYN WAUGH

D1638204

EVELYN WAUGH

The Ordeal of Gilbert Pinfold
Tactical Exercise
Love Among the Ruins

*

PENGUIN BOOKS

Penguin Books Ltd, Harmondsworth, Middlesex
AUSTRALIA: Penguin Books Pty Ltd, 762 Whitehorse Road,
Mitcham, Victoria

—

The Ordeal of Gilbert Pinfold first published by
Chapman & Hall 1957
Tactical Exercise first published by
Penguin Books 1962
Love Among the Ruins first published by
Chapman & Hall 1953
Published in one volume by Penguin Books 1962

—

Copyright © Evelyn Waugh, 1962

—

Made and printed in Great Britain
by Cox and Wyman Ltd,
London, Reading, and Fakenham
Set in Monotype Bembo

This book is sold subject to the condition
that it shall not, by way of trade, be lent,
re-sold, hired out, or otherwise disposed
of without the publisher's consent,
in any form of binding or cover
other than that in which
it is published

Contents

The Ordeal of Gilbert Pinfold

A CONVERSATION PIECE

TO DAPHNE

IN THE CONFIDENCE

THAT HER ABOUNDING SYMPATHY

WILL EXTEND EVEN TO

POOR PINFOLD

I

PORTRAIT OF THE ARTIST IN
MIDDLE-AGE

IT may happen in the next hundred years that the English novelists of the present day will come to be valued as we now value the artists and craftsmen of the late eighteenth century. The originators, the exuberant men, are extinct and in their place subsists and modestly flourishes a generation notable for elegance and variety of contrivance. It may well happen that there are lean years ahead in which our posterity will look back hungrily to this period, when there was so much will and so much ability to please.

Among these novelists Mr Gilbert Pinfold stood quite high. At the time of his adventure, at the age of fifty, he had written a dozen books all of which were still bought and read. They were translated into most languages and in the United States of America enjoyed intermittent but lucrative seasons of favour. Foreign students often chose them as the subject for theses, but those who sought to detect cosmic significance in Mr Pinfold's work, to relate it to fashions in philosophy, social predicaments, or psychological tensions, were baffled by his frank, curt replies to their questionnaires; their fellows in the English Literature School, who chose more egotistical writers, often found their theses more than half composed for them. Mr Pinfold gave nothing away. Not that he was secretive or grudging by nature; he had nothing to give these students. He regarded his books as objects which he had made, things quite external to himself to be used and judged by others. He thought them well made, better than many reputed works of genius, but he was not vain of his accomplishment, still less of his reputation. He had no wish to obliterate anything he had written, but he would dearly have liked to revise it, envying painters, who are allowed to return to the same theme time and time again, clarifying and enriching until they have done all they can with it. A novelist is condemned to produce a succession of novelties, new names for characters, new incidents for his plots, new scenery; but, Mr Pinfold maintained, most men harbour the germs of one or two books only; all else is professional trickery of which the most daemonic of the masters – Dickens and Balzac even – were flagrantly guilty.

At the beginning of this fifty-first year of his life Mr Pinfold presented to the world most of the attributes of well-being. Affectionate, high-spirited, and busy in childhood; dissipated and often despairing in youth; sturdy and prosperous in early manhood; he had in middle-age degenerated less than many of his contemporaries. He attributed this superiority to his long, lonely, tranquil days at Lychpole, a secluded village some hundred miles from London.

He was devoted to a wife many years younger than himself, who actively farmed the small property. Their children were numerous, healthy, good-looking, and good-mannered, and his income just sufficed for their education. Once he had travelled widely; now he spent most of the year in the shabby old house which, over the years, he had filled with pictures and books and furniture of the kind he relished. As a soldier he had sustained, in good heart, much discomfort and some danger. Since the end of the war his life had been strictly private. In his own village he took very lightly the duties which he might have thought incumbent on him. He contributed adequate sums to local causes but he had no interest in sport or in local government, no ambition to lead or to command. He had never voted in a parliamentary election, maintaining an idiosyncratic toryism which was quite unrepresented in the political parties of his time and was regarded by his neighbours as being almost as sinister as socialism.

These neighbours were typical of the English countryside of the period. A few rich men farmed commercially on a large scale; a few had business elsewhere and came home merely to hunt; the majority were elderly and in reduced circumstances; people who, when the Pinfolds settled at Lychpole, lived comfortably with servants and horses, and now lived in much smaller houses and met at the fishmonger's. Many of these were related to one another, and formed a compact little clan. Colonel and Mrs Bagnold, Mr and Mrs Graves, Mrs and Miss Fawdle, Colonel and Miss Garbett, Lady Fawdle-Upton, and Miss Clarissa Bagnold all lived in a radius of ten miles from Lychpole. All were in some way related. In the first years of their marriage Mr and Mrs Pinfold had dined in all these households and had entertained them in return. But after the war the decline of fortune, less sharp in the Pinfolds' case than their neighbours', made their meetings less frequent. The Pinfolds were addicted to nicknames and each of these surrounding families had its own private, unsuspected appellation at Lychpole, not malicious but mildly derisive, taking its origin in most cases from some half-forgotten incident in the past. The nearest neighbour whom they saw most often was Reginald Graves-Upton, an uncle of the Graves-Uptons ten miles distant at Upper Mewling; a gentle, bee-keeping old bachelor who inhabited a thatched cottage up the lane less than a mile from the Manor. It was his habit on Sunday mornings to walk to church across the Pinfolds' fields and leave his Cairn terrier in the Pinfolds' stables while he attended Matins. He called for quarter of an hour when he came to fetch his dog,

drank a small glass of sherry, and described the wireless pro-
grammes he had heard during the preceding week. This
refined, fastidious old gentleman went by the recondite name
of 'the Bruiser', sometimes varied to 'Pug', 'Basher', and
'Old Fisticuffs', all of which sobriquets derived from 'Boxer';
for in recent years he had added to his few interests an object
which he reverently referred to as 'The Box'.

This Box was one of many operating in various parts of
the country. It was installed under the sceptical noses of
Reginald Graves-Upton's nephew and niece, at Upper Mewling. Mrs Pinfold, who had been taken to see it, said it looked
like a makeshift wireless-set. According to the Bruiser and
other devotees The Box exercised diagnostic and therapeutic
powers. Some part of a sick man or animal – a hair, a drop of
blood preferably – was brought to The Box, whose guardian
would then 'tune in' to the 'life-waves' of the patient, discern
the origin of the malady and prescribe treatment.

Mr Pinfold was as sceptical as the younger Graves-Uptons.
Mrs Pinfold thought there must be something in it, because
it had been tried, without her knowledge, on Lady Fawdle-
Upton's nettle-rash and immediate relief had followed.

'It's all suggestion,' said young Mrs Graves-Upton.

'It can't be suggestion, if she didn't know it was being
done,' said Mr Pinfold.

'No. It's simply a matter of measuring the Life-Waves,' said
Mrs Pinfold.

'An extremely dangerous device in the wrong hands,' said
Mr Pinfold.

'No, no. That is the beauty of it. It can't do any harm. You
see it only transmits *Life* Forces. Fanny Graves tried it on her
spaniel for worms, but they simply grew enormous with all
the Life Force going into them. Like serpents, Fanny said.'

'I should have thought this Box counted as sorcery,' Mr

Pinfold said to his wife when they were alone. 'You ought to confess it.'

'D'you really think so?'

'No, not really. It's just a lot of harmless nonsense.'

The Pinfolds' religion made a slight but perceptible barrier between them and these neighbours, a large part of whose activities centred round their parish churches. The Pinfolds were Roman Catholics, Mrs Pinfold by upbringing, Mr Pinfold by a later development. He had been received into the Church – 'conversion' suggests an event more sudden and emotional than his calm acceptance of the propositions of his faith – in early manhood, at the time when many Englishmen of humane education were falling into communism. Unlike them Mr Pinfold remained steadfast. But he was reputed bigoted rather than pious. His trade by its nature is liable to the condemnation of the clergy as, at the best, frivolous; at the worst, corrupting. Moreover by the narrow standards of the age his habits of life were self-indulgent and his uttterances lacked prudence. And at the very time when the leaders of his Church were exhorting their people to emerge from the catacombs into the forum, to make their influence felt in democratic politics and to regard worship as a corporate rather than a private act, Mr Pinfold burrowed ever deeper into the rock. Away from his parish he sought the least frequented Mass; at home he held aloof from the multifarious organizations which have sprung into being at the summons of the hierarchy to redeem the times.

But Mr Pinfold was far from friendless and he set great store by his friends. They were the men and women who were growing old with him, whom in the nineteen-twenties and thirties he had seen constantly; who in the diaspora of the forties and fifties kept more tenuous touch with one another, the men at Bellamy's Club, the women at the half-dozen poky, pretty houses of Westminster and Belgravia to which had descended the larger hospitality of a happier age.

He had made no new friends in late years. Sometimes he thought he detected a slight coldness among his old cronies. It was always he, it seemed to him, who proposed a meeting. It was always they who first rose to leave. In particular there was one, Roger Stillingfleet, who had once been an intimate but now seemed to avoid him. Roger Stillingfleet was a writer, one of the few Mr Pinfold really liked. He knew of no reason for their estrangement and, inquiring, was told that Roger had grown very odd lately. He never came to Bellamy's now, it was said, except to collect his letters or to entertain a visiting American.

It sometimes occurred to Mr Pinfold that he must be growing into a bore. His opinions certainly were easily predictable.

His strongest tastes were negative. He abhorred plastics, Picasso, sunbathing, and jazz – everything in fact that had happened in his own lifetime. The tiny kindling of charity which came to him through his religion sufficed only to temper his disgust and change it to boredom. There was a phrase in the thirties: 'It is later than you think', which was designed to cause uneasiness. It was never later than Mr Pinfold thought. At intervals during the day and night he would look at his watch and learn always with disappointment how little of his life was past, how much there was still ahead of him. He wished no one ill, but he looked at the world *sub specie aeternitatis* and he found it flat as a map; except when, rather often, personal annoyance intruded. Then he would come tumbling from his exalted point of observation. Shocked by a bad bottle of wine, an impertinent stranger, or a fault in syntax, his mind like a cinema camera trucked furiously forward to confront the offending object close-up with glaring lens; with the eyes of a drill sergeant inspecting an awkward squad, bulging with wrath that was half-facetious, and with half-simulated incredulity; like a drill sergeant he was absurd to many but to some rather formidable.

Once upon a time all this had been thought diverting. People quoted his pungent judgements and invented anecdotes of his audacity, which were recounted as 'typical Pinfolds'. Now, he realized his singularity had lost some of its attraction for others, but he was too old a dog to learn new tricks.

As a boy, at the age of puberty when most of his school-fellows coarsened, he had been as fastidious as the Bruiser and in his early years of success diffidence had lent him charm. Prolonged prosperity had wrought the change. He had seen sensitive men make themselves a protective disguise against the rebuffs and injustices of manhood. Mr Pinfold had suffered little in these ways; he had been tenderly reared and, as a writer, welcomed and over-rewarded early. It was his modesty which needed protection and for this purpose, but without design, he gradually assumed this character of burlesque. He was neither a scholar nor a regular soldier; the part for which he cast himself was a combination of eccentric don and testy colonel and he acted it strenuously, before his children at Lychpole and his cronies in London, until it came to dominate his whole outward personality. When he ceased to be alone, when he swung into his club or stumped up the nursery stairs, he left half of himself behind, and the other half swelled to fill its place. He offered the world a front of pomposity mitigated by indiscretion, that was as hard, bright, and antiquated as a cuirass.

Mr Pinfold's nanny used to say: 'Don't care went to the gallows'; also: 'Sticks and stones can break my bones, but words can never hurt me'. Mr Pinfold did not care what the village or his neighbours said of him. As a little boy he had been acutely sensitive to ridicule. His adult shell seemed impervious. He had long held himself inaccessible to interviewers and the young men and women who were employed to write 'profiles' collected material where they could. Every week his press-cutting agents brought to his breakfast-table two or three rather offensive allusions. He accepted without much resentment the world's estimate of himself. It was part of the price he paid for privacy. There were also letters from strangers, some abusive, some adulatory. Mr Pinfold was unable to discover any particular superiority of taste or expression in the writers of either sort. To both he sent printed acknowledgements.

His days passed in writing, reading, and managing his own small affairs. He had never employed a secretary and for the last two years he had been without a manservant. But Mr Pinfold did not repine. He was perfectly competent to answer his own letters, pay his bills, tie his parcels, and fold his clothes. At night his most frequent recurring dream was of doing *The Times* crossword puzzle; his most disagreeable that he was reading a tedious book aloud to his family.

Physically, in his late forties, he had become lazy. Time was, he rode to hounds, went for long walks, dug his garden, felled small trees. Now he spent most of the day in an armchair. He ate less, drank more, and grew corpulent. He was very seldom so ill as to spend a day in bed. He suffered intermittently from various twinges and brief bouts of pain in his joints and muscles – arthritis, gout, rheumatism, fibrositis; they were not dignified by any scientific name. Mr Pinfold seldom consulted his doctor. When he did so it was as a 'private patient'. His children availed themselves of the National Health Act but Mr Pinfold was reluctant to disturb a relationship which had been formed in his first years at Lychpole. Dr Drake,

Mr Pinfold's medical attendant, had inherited the practice from his father and had been there before the Pinfolds came to Lychpole. Lean, horsy, and weather-beaten in appearance, he had deep roots and wide ramifications in the countryside, being brother of the local auctioneer, brother-in-law of the solicitor and cousin of three neighbouring rectors. His recreations were sporting. He was not a man of high technical pretensions but he suited Mr Pinfold well. He too suffered, more sharply, from Mr Pinfold's troubles and when consulted remarked that Mr Pinfold must expect these things at his age, that the whole district was afflicted in this way and that Lychpole was notoriously the worst spot in it.

Mr Pinfold also slept badly. It was a trouble of long standing. For twenty-five years he had used various sedatives, for the last ten years a single specific, chloral and bromide which, unknown to Dr Drake, he bought on an old prescription in London. There were periods of literary composition when he would find the sentences he had written during the day running in his head, the words shifting and changing colour kaleidoscopically, so that he would again and again climb out of bed, pad down to the library, make a minute correction, return to his room, lie in the dark dazzled by the pattern of vocables until obliged once more to descend to the manuscript. But those days and nights of obsession, of what might without vainglory be called 'creative' work, were a small part of his year. On most nights he was neither fretful nor apprehensive. He was merely bored. After even the idlest day he demanded six or seven hours of insensibility. With them behind him, with them to look forward to, he could face another idle day with something approaching jauntiness; and these his doses unfailingly provided.

At about the time of his fiftieth birthday there occurred

two events which seemed trivial at the time but grew to importance in his later adventures.

The first of these primarily concerned Mrs Pinfold. During the war Lychpole was let, the house to a convent, the fields to a grazier. This man, Hill, had collected parcels of grass-land in and around the parish and on them kept a nondescript herd of 'unattested' dairy-cattle. The pasture was rank, the fences dilapidated.When the Pinfolds came home in 1945 and wanted their fields back, the War Agricultural Committee, normally predisposed towards the sitting tenant, were in no doubt of their decision in Mrs Pinfold's favour. Had she acted at once, Hill would have been out, with his compensation, at Michaelmas, but Mrs Pinfold was tender-hearted and Hill was adroit. First he pleaded, then, having established new rights, asserted them. Lady Day succeeded Michaelmas; Michaelmas, Lady Day for four full years. Hill retreated meadow by meadow. The committee, still popularly known as 'the War Ag.', returned, walked the property anew, again found for Mrs Pinfold. Hill, who now had a lawyer, appealed. So it went on. Mr Pinfold held aloof from it all, merely noting with sorrow the anxiety of his wife. At length at Michaelmas 1949 Hill finally moved. He boasted in the village inn of his cleverness, and left for the other side of the county with a comfortable profit.

The second event occurred soon after. Mr Pinfold received an invitation from the B.B.C. to record an 'interview'. In the previous twenty years there had been many such proposals and he had always refused them. This time the fee was more liberal and the conditions softer. He would not have to go to the offices in London. Electricians would come to him with their apparatus. No script had to be submitted; no preparation of any kind was required; the whole thing would take an hour. In an idle moment Mr Pinfold agreed and at once regretted it.

The day came towards the end of the summer holidays. Soon after breakfast there arrived a motor-car, and a van of the sort used in the army by the more important kinds of signaller, which immediately absorbed the attention of the younger children. Out of the car there came three youngish men, thin of hair, with horn-rimmed elliptical glasses, cord trousers, and tweed coats; exactly what Mr Pinfold was expecting. Their leader was named Angel. He emphasized his primacy by means of a neat, thick beard. He and his colleagues, he explained, had slept in the district, where he had an aunt. They would have to leave before luncheon. They would get through their business in the morning. The signallers began rapidly uncoiling wires and setting up their microphone in the library, while Mr Pinfold drew the attention of Angel and his party to the more noticeable of his collection of works of art. They did not commit themselves to an opinion, merely remarking that the last house they visited had a gouache by Rouault.

'I didn't know he ever painted in gouache,' said Mr Pinfold. 'Anyway he's a dreadful painter.'

'Ah!' said Angel. 'That's very nice. Very nice indeed. We must try and work that into the broadcast.'

When the electricians had made their arrangements Mr Pinfold sat at his table with the three strangers, a microphone in their midst. They were attempting to emulate a series that had been cleverly done in Paris with various French celebrities, in which informal, spontaneous discussion had seduced the objects of inquiry into self-revelation.

They questioned Mr Pinfold in turn about his tastes and habits. Angel led and it was at him that Mr Pinfold looked. The commonplace face above the beard became slightly sinister, the accentless, but insidiously plebeian voice, menacing. The questions were civil enough in form but Mr Pinfold thought he could detect an underlying malice. Angel seemed to believe that anyone sufficiently eminent to be interviewed by him must have something to hide, must be an impostor whom it was his business to trap and expose, and to direct his questions from some basic, previous knowledge of something discreditable. There was the hint of the under-dog's snarl which Mr Pinfold recognized from his press-cuttings.

He was well equipped to deal with insolence, real or imagined, and answered succinctly and shrewdly, disconcerting his adversaries, if adversaries they were, point by point. When it was over Mr Pinfold offered his visitors sherry. Tension relaxed. He asked politely who was their next subject.

'We're going on to Stratford,' said Angel, 'to interview Cedric Thorne.'

'You evidently have not seen this morning's paper,' said Mr Pinfold.

'No, we left before it came.'

'Cedric Thorne has escaped you. He hanged himself yesterday afternoon in his dressing-room.'

'Good heavens, are you sure?'

'It's in *The Times*.'

'May I see?'

Angel was shaken from his professional calm. Mr Pinfold brought the paper and he read the paragraph with emotion.

'Yes, yes. That's him. I half expected this. He was a personal friend. I must get on to his wife. May I phone?'

Mr Pinfold apologized for the levity with which he had broken the news and led Angel to the business-room. He refilled the sherry glasses and attempted to appear genial. Angel returned shortly to say: 'I couldn't get through. I'll have to try again later.'

Mr Pinfold repeated his regrets.

'Yes, it is a terrible thing – not wholly unexpected though.'

A macabre note had been added to the discords of the morning.

Then hands were shaken; the vehicles turned on the gravel and drove away.

When they were out of sight down the turn of the drive, one of the children who had been listening to the conversation in the van said: 'You didn't like those people much, did you, papa?'

He had definitely not liked them and they left an unpleasant memory which grew sharper in the weeks before the record was broadcast. He brooded. It seemed to him that an attempt had been made against his privacy and he was not sure how effectively he had defended it. He strained to remember his precise words and his memory supplied various distorted versions. Finally the evening came when the performance was made public. Mr Pinfold had the cook's wireless carried into the drawing-room. He and Mrs Pinfold listened together. His voice came to him strangely old and fruity, but what he said gave him no regret. 'They tried to make an ass of me,' he said. 'I don't believe they succeeded.'

Mr Pinfold for the time forgot Angel.

Boredom alone and some stiffness in the joints disturbed that sunny autumn. Despite his age and dangerous trade Mr Pinfold seemed to himself and to others unusually free of the fashionable agonies of *angst*.

2

COLLAPSE OF ELDERLY PARTY

MR PINFOLD's idleness has been remarked. He was half-way through a novel and had stopped work in early summer. The completed chapters had been typed, rewritten, retyped, and lay in a drawer of his desk. He was entirely satisfied with them. He knew in a general way what had to be done to finish the book and he believed he could at any moment set himself to do it. But he was not pressed for money. The sales of his earlier works had already earned him that year the modest sufficiency which the laws of his country allowed. Further effort could only bring him sharply diminishing rewards and he was disinclined to effort. It was as though the characters he had quickened had fallen into a light doze and he left them benevolently to themselves. Hard things were in store for them. Let them sleep while they could. All his life he had worked intermittently. In youth his long periods of leisure had been devoted to amusement. Now he had abandoned that quest. That was the main difference between Mr Pinfold at fifty and Mr Pinfold at thirty.

Winter set in sharp at the end of October. The central-heating plant at Lychpole was ancient and voracious. It had not been used since the days of fuel shortage. With most of the children away at school Mr and Mrs Pinfold withdrew into two rooms, heaped the fires with such coal as they could procure, and sheltered from draughts behind screens and sand-bags. Mr Pinfold's spirits sank, he began to talk of the West Indies and felt the need of longer periods of sleep.

The composition of his sleeping-draught, as originally prescribed, was largely of water. He suggested to his chemist that it would save trouble to have the essential ingredients in full strength and to dilute them himself. Their taste was bitter and after various experiments he found they were most palatable in crème de menthe. He was not scrupulous in measuring the dose. He splashed into the glass as much as his mood suggested and if he took too little and woke in the small hours he would get out of bed and make unsteadily for the bottles and a second swig. Thus he passed many hours in welcome unconsciousness; but all was not well with him. Whether from too much strong medicine or from some other cause, he felt decidedly seedy by the middle of November. He found himself disagreeably flushed, particularly after drinking his normal, not illiberal, quantity of wine and brandy. Crimson blotches appeared on the backs of his hands.

He called in Dr Drake who said: 'That sounds like an allergy.'

'Allergic to what?'

'Ah, that's hard to say. Almost anything can cause an allergy nowadays. It might be something you're wearing or some plant growing near. The only cure really is a change.'

'I might go abroad after Christmas.'

'Yes, that's the best thing you could do. Anyway don't worry. No one ever died of an allergy. It's allied to hay-fever,' he added learnedly, 'and asthma.'

Another thing which troubled him and which he soon began to attribute to his medicine was the behaviour of his memory. It began to play him tricks. He did not grow forgetful. He remembered everything in clear detail but he remembered it wrong. He would state a fact, dogmatically, sometimes in print – a date, a name, a quotation – find himself challenged, turn to his books for verification and find most disconcertingly that he was at fault.

Two incidents of this kind slightly alarmed him. With the idea of cheering him up Mrs Pinfold invited a week-end party to Lychpole. On the Sunday afternoon he proposed a visit to a remarkable tomb in a neighbouring church. He had not been there since the war, but he had a clear image of it, which he described to them in technical detail; a recumbent figure of the mid sixteenth century in gilded bronze; something almost unique in England. They found the place without difficulty; it was unquestionably what they sought; but the figure was of coloured alabaster. They laughed, he laughed, but he was shocked.

The second incident was more humiliating. A friend in London, James Lance, who shared his tastes in furniture, found, and offered him as a present, a most remarkable piece; a wash-hand stand of the greatest elaboration designed by an English architect of the 1860s, a man not universally honoured but of magisterial status to Mr Pinfold and his friends. This massive freak of fancy was decorated with metal work and mosaic, and with a series of panels painted in his hot youth by a rather preposterous artist who later became President of the Royal Academy. It was just such a trophy as Mr Pinfold most valued. He hurried to London, studied the object with exultation, arranged for its delivery, and impatiently awaited its arrival at Lychpole. A fortnight later it came, was borne upstairs and set in the space cleared for it. Then to his horror Mr Pinfold observed that an essential part was missing. There should have been a prominent, highly ornamental, copper tap in the centre, forming the climax of the design. In its place there was merely a small socket. Mr Pinfold broke into lamentation. The carriers asserted that this was the condition of the piece when they fetched it. Mr Pinfold bade them search their van. Nothing was found. Mr Pinfold surcharged the receipt 'incomplete' and immediately wrote to the firm ordering a diligent search of the ware-house where the wash-hand stand had reposed *en route* and enclosing a detailed drawing of the lost member. There was a brisk exchange of letters, the carriers denying all responsibility. Finally Mr Pinfold, decently reluctant to involve the donor in a dispute about a gift, wrote to James Lance asking for corroboration. James Lance replied: there never had been any tap such as Mr Pinfold described.

'You haven't always been altogether making sense lately,' said Mrs Pinfold when her husband showed her this letter, 'and you're a very odd colour. Either you're drinking too much or doping too much, or both.'

'I wonder if you're right,' said Mr Pinfold. 'Perhaps I ought to go slow after Christmas.'

The children's holidays were a time when Mr Pinfold felt a special need for unconsciousness at night and for stimulated geniality by day. Christmas was always the worst season. During that dread week he made copious use of wine and narcotics and his inflamed face shone like the florid squireens depicted in the cards that littered the house. Once catching sight of himself in the looking-glass, thus empurpled and wearing a paper crown, he took fright at what he saw.

'I *must* get away,' said Mr Pinfold later to his wife. 'I must go somewhere sunny and finish my book.'

'I wish I could come too. There's so much to be done getting Hill's horrible fields back into shape. I'm rather worried about you, you know. You ought to have someone to look after you.'

'I'll be all right. I work better alone.'

The cold grew intense. Mr Pinfold spent the day crouched over the library fire. To leave it for the icy passages made him shudder and stumble, half benumbed, while outside the hidden sun glared over a landscape that seemed all turned to metal; lead and iron and steel. Only in the evenings did Mr Pinfold manage a semblance of jollity, joining his family in charades or Up Jenkins, playing the fool to the loud delight of the youngest and the tolerant amusement of the eldest of his children, until in degrees of age they went happily to their rooms and he was released into his own darkness and silence.

At length the holidays came to an end. Nuns and monks received their returning charges and Lychpole was left in peace save for rare intrusions from the nursery. And now just when Mr Pinfold was gathering himself as it were for a strenuous effort at reformation, he was struck down by the most severe attack of his 'aches' which he had yet suffered. Every joint, but especially feet, ankles, and knees, agonized him. Dr Drake again advocated a warm climate and prescribed some pills which he said were 'something new and pretty powerful'. They were large and drab, reminding Mr Pinfold of the pellets of blotting-paper which used to be rolled at his private school. Mr Pinfold added them to his bromide and chloral and crème de menthe, his wine and gin and brandy, and to a new sleeping-draught which his doctor, ignorant of the existence of his other bottle, also supplied.

And now his mind became much overcast. One great thought excluded all others, the need to escape. He, who even in this extremity eschewed the telephone, telegraphed to the travel-agency with whom he dealt: *Kindly arrange immediate passage West Indies, East Indies, Africa, India, anywhere hot, luxury preferred, private bath, outside single cabin essential*, and anxiously awaited the reply. When it came it comprised a large envelope full of decorative folders and a note saying they awaited his further instructions.

Mr Pinfold became frantic. He knew one of the directors of the firm. He thought he had met others. It came to him in his daze quite erroneously that he had lately read somewhere that a lady of his acquaintance had joined the board. To all of them at their private addresses he dispatched peremptory telegrams: *Kindly investigate wanton inefficiency your office. Pinfold.*

The director whom he really knew took action. There was little choice at that moment. Mr Pinfold was lucky to secure a passage in the *Caliban*, a one-class ship sailing in three days for Ceylon.

During the time of waiting Mr Pinfold's frenzy subsided. He became instead intermittently comatose. When lucid he was in pain.

Mrs Pinfold said, as she had often said before: 'You're doped, darling, up to the eyes.'

'Yes. It's those rheumatism pills. Drake said they were very strong.'

Mr Pinfold, who was normally rather deft, now became clumsy. He dropped things. He found his buttons and laces intractable, his handwriting in the few letters which his journey necessitated, uncertain, his spelling, never strong, wildly barbaric.

In one of his clearer hours he said to Mrs Pinfold: 'I believe you are right. I shall give up the sleeping-draughts as soon as I get to sea. I always sleep better at sea. I shall cut down on drink too. As soon as I get rid of these damned aches, I shall start work. I can always work at sea. I shall have the book finished before I get home.'

These resolutions persisted; there was a sober, industrious time ahead of him in a few days' time. He had to survive somehow until then. Everything would come right very soon.

Mrs Pinfold shared these hopes. She was busy with her plans for the farm which the newly liberated territory made more elaborate. She could not get away. Nor did she think her presence was needed. Once her husband was safely on board, all would be well with him.

She helped him pack. Indeed he could do nothing except sit on a bedroom chair and give confused directions. He must take foolscap paper, he said, in large quantities; also ink, foreign ink was never satisfactory. And pens. He had once experienced great difficulty in New York in purchasing pennibs; he had in the end had recourse to a remote law-stationer's. All foreigners, he was now convinced, used some kind of stylographic instrument. He must take pens and nibs. His clothes were a matter of indifference. You could always get a Chinaman, anywhere out of Europe, to make you a suit of clothes in an afternoon, Mr Pinfold said.

That Sunday morning Mr Pinfold did not go to Mass. He lay in bed until midday and, when he came down, hobbled to the drawing-room window and gazed across the bare, icy park thinking of the welcoming tropics. Then he said: 'Oh God, here comes the Bruiser.'

'Hide.'

'No fire in the library.'

'I'll tell him you're ill.'

'No. I like the Bruiser. Besides, if you say I'm ill, he'll set his damned Box to work on me.'

Throughout the short visit Mr Pinfold exerted himself to be affable.

'You aren't looking at all well, Gilbert,' the Bruiser said.

'I'm all right really. A twinge of rheumatism. I'm sailing the day after tomorrow for Ceylon.'

'That's very sudden, isn't it?'

'The weather. Need a change.'

He sank into his chair and then, when the Bruiser left, got to his feet again with an enormous obvious effort.

'Please don't come out,' said the Bruiser.

Mrs Pinfold went with him to release his dog and when she returned found Mr Pinfold enraged.

'I know what you two have been talking about.'

'Do you? I was hearing about the Fawdles' row with the Parish Council about their right of way.'

'You've been giving him my hair for his Box.'

'Nonsense, Gilbert.'

'I could tell by the way he looked at me that he was measuring my Life-Waves.'

Mrs Pinfold looked at him sadly. 'You really are in rather a bad way, aren't you, darling?'

The *Caliban* was not a ship so large as to require a special train; carriages were reserved on the regular service from London. Mrs Pinfold accompanied him there the day before his departure. He had to collect his tickets from the travel-agency, but when he arrived in London great lassitude came over him and he went straight to bed in his hotel, summoning a messenger from the agency to bring them to him. A young, polite man came at once. He bore a small portfolio of documents, tickets for train and ship and for return by air, baggage forms, embarkation cards, carbon copies of letters of reservation, and the like. Mr Pinfold had difficulty in understanding. He had trouble with his cheque book. The young man looked at him with more than normal curiosity. Perhaps he was a reader of Mr Pinfold's works. It was more probable that he found something bizarre in the spectacle of Mr Pinfold, lying there groaning and muttering, propped by pillows, purple in the face, with a bottle of champagne open beside him. Mr Pinfold offered him a glass. He refused. When he had gone Mr Pinfold said: 'I didn't at all like the look of that young man.'

'Oh, he was all right,' said Mrs Pinfold.

'There was something fishy about him,' said Mr Pinfold.
'He stared at me as though he was measuring my Life-Waves.'

Then he fell into a doze.

Mrs Pinfold lunched alone downstairs and rejoined her
husband who said: 'I must go and say good-bye to my mother.
Order a car.'

'Darling, you aren't well enough.'

'I *always* say good-bye to her before going abroad. I've
told her we are coming.'

'I'll telephone and explain. Or shall I go out there alone?'

'I'm going. It's true I'm not well enough, but I'm going.
Get the hall-porter to have a car here in half an hour.'

Mr Pinfold's widowed mother lived in a pretty little house
at Kew. She was eighty-two years old, sharp of sight and
hearing, but of recent years very slow of mind. In childhood
Mr Pinfold had loved her extravagantly. There remained
now only a firm *pietas*. He no longer enjoyed her company
nor wished to communicate. She had been left rather badly
off by his father. Mr Pinfold supplemented her income with
payments under a deed of covenant so that she was now comfortably placed with a single, faithful old maid to look after
her and all her favourite possessions, preserved from the larger
house, set out round her. Young Mrs Pinfold, who would
talk happily of her children, was very much more agreeable
company to the old woman than was her son, but Mr Pinfold
went to call dutifully several times a year and, as he said,
always before an absence of any length.

A funereal limousine bore them to Kew. Mr Pinfold sat
huddled in rugs. He hobbled on two sticks, one a blackthorn,
the other a malacca cane, through the little gate up the garden
path. An hour later he was out again, subsiding with groans
into the back of the car. The visit had not been a success.

'It wasn't a success, was it?' said Mr Pinfold.

'We ought to have stayed to tea.'

'She knows I never have tea.'

'But I do, and Mrs Yercombe had it all prepared. I saw it on a trolley – cakes and sandwiches and a muffin-dish.'

'The truth is my mother doesn't like to see anyone younger than herself iller than herself – except children of course.'

'You were beastly snubbing about the children.'

'Yes. I know. Damn. Damn. Damn. I'll write to her from the ship. I'll send her a cable. Why does everyone except me find it so easy to be nice?'

When he reached the hotel he returned to bed and ordered another bottle of champagne. He dozed again. Mrs Pinfold sat quietly reading a paper-covered detective story. He awoke and ordered a rather elaborate dinner, but by the time it came his appetite was gone. Mrs Pinfold ate well, but sadly. When the table was wheeled out, Mr Pinfold hobbled to the bathroom and took his blue-grey pills. Three a day was the number prescribed. He had a dozen left. He took a big dose of his sleeping-draught; the bottle was half full.

'I'm taking too much,' he said, not for the first time. 'I'll finish what I've got and never order any more.' He looked at himself in the glass. He looked at the backs of his hands which were again mottled with large crimson patches. 'I'm sure it's not really good for me,' he said, and felt his way to bed, tumbled in, and fell heavily asleep.

His train was at ten next day. The funereal limousine was ordered. Mr Pinfold dressed laboriously and, without shaving, went to the station. Mrs Pinfold came with him. He needed help to find a porter and to find his seat. He dropped his ticket and his sticks on the platform.

'I don't believe you ought to be going alone,' said Mrs Pinfold. 'Wait for another ship and I'll come too.'

'No, no. I shall be all right.'

But some hours later when he reached the docks Mr Pinfold did not feel so hopeful. He had slept most of the way, now and then waking to light a cigar and let it fall from his fingers after a few puffs. His aches seemed sharper than ever as he climbed out of the carriage. Snow was falling. The distance from the train to the ship seemed enormous. The other passengers stepped out briskly. Mr Pinfold moved slowly. On the quay a telegraph boy was taking messages. Mrs Pinfold would be back at Lychpole by now. Mr Pinfold with great difficulty wrote: *Safely embarked. All love.* Then he moved to the gangway and painfully climbed aboard.

A coloured steward led him to his cabin. He gazed round it unseeing, sitting on a bunk. There was something he ought to do; telegraph his mother. On the cabin table was some writing paper bearing the ship's name and the flag of the line at its head. Mr Pinfold tried to compose and inscribe a message. The task proved to be one of insuperable difficulty. He threw the spoilt paper into the basket and sat on his bed, still in his hat and overcoat with his sticks beside him. Presently his two suitcases arrived. He gazed at them for some time, then began to unpack. That too proved difficult. He rang his bell and the coloured steward reappeared bowing and smiling.

'I'm not very well. I wonder if you could unpack for me?'

'Dinner seven-thirty o'clock, sir.'

'I said, could you unpack for me?'

'No, sir, bar not open in port, sir.'

The man smiled and bowed and left Mr Pinfold.

Mr Pinfold sat there, in his hat and coat, holding his cudgel and his cane. Presently an English steward appeared with the passenger list, some forms to fill, and the message: 'The Captain's compliments, sir, and he would like to have the honour of your company at his table in the dining-saloon.'

'Now?'

'No, sir. Dinner is at 7.30. I don't expect the Captain will be dining in the saloon tonight.'

'I don't think I shall either,' said Mr Pinfold. 'Thank the Captain. Very civil of him. Another night. Someone said something about the bar not being open. Can't you get me some brandy?'

'Oh yes, sir. I think so, sir. Any particular brand?'

'Brandy,' said Mr Pinfold. 'Large one.'

The chief steward brought it with his own hands.

'Good night,' said Mr Pinfold.

He found on the top of his case the things he needed for the night. Among them his pills and his bottle. The brandy impelled him to action. He must telegraph to his mother. He groped his way out and along the corridor to the purser's office. A clerk was on duty, very busy with his papers behind a grill.

'I want to send a telegram.'

'Yes, sir. There's a boy at the head of the gangway.'

'I'm not feeling very well. I wonder if you could be very kind and write it for me?'

The purser looked at him hard, observed his unshaven chin, smelled brandy, and drew on his long experience of travellers.

'Sorry about that, sir. Pleased to be any help.'

Mr Pinfold dictated, *'Everyone in ship most helpful. Love, Gilbert,'* fumbled with a handful of silver, then crept back to his cabin. There he took his large grey pills and a swig of his sleeping-draught. Then, prayerless, he got himself to bed.

3

AN UNHAPPY SHIP

THE S.S *Caliban*, Captain Steerforth master, was middle-aged and middle-class; clean, trustworthy and comfortable, without pretence to luxury. There were no private baths. Meals were not served in cabins, it was stated, except on the orders of the medical officer. Her public rooms were panelled in fumed oak in the fashion of an earlier generation. She plied between Liverpool and Rangoon, stopping at intermediate ports, carrying a mixed cargo and a more or less homogeneous company of passengers, Scotchmen and their wives mostly, travelling on business and on leave. Crew and stewards were Lascars.

When Mr Pinfold came to himself it was full day and he was rocking gently to and fro in his narrow bed with the slow roll of the high seas.

He had barely noticed his cabin on the preceding evening. Now he observed that it was a large one, with two berths. There was a little window made of slats of opaque glass, fitted with tight, ornamental muslin curtains, and a sliding shutter. This gave, not on the sea, but on a deck where people from time to time passed, casting a brief shadow but with no sound that was audible above the beat of the engine, the regular creak of plates and woodwork, and the continuous insect-hum of the ventilator. The ceiling, at which Mr Pinfold gazed, was spanned as though by a cottage beam by a white studded air-shaft and by a multiplicity of pipes and electric cable. Mr Pinfold lay for some time gazing and rocking, not quite sure where he was, but rather pleased than not to be there. His watch, unwound the night before, had run down. He had been called. On the shelf at his side a cup of tea, already quite cold, slopped in its saucer, and beside it, stained with spilt tea, was the ship's passenger list. He found himself entered as *Mr G. Penfold* and thought of Mr Pooter at the Mansion House. The misprint was welcome as an item of disguise, an uncovenanted addition to his privacy. He glanced idly through the other names – '*Dr Abercrombie, Mr Addison, Miss Amory, Mr and Mrs and Miss Margaret Angel, Mr and Mrs Benson, Mr Blackadder, Major and Mrs Cockson*', no one he knew, no one likely to annoy him. There were half a dozen Burmese on their way to Rangoon; the rest were solidly British. No one, he felt confident, would have read his books or would seek to draw him into literary conversation. He would be able to do a quiet three weeks' work in this ship as soon as his health mended.

He sat up and put his feet to the floor. He was still crippled but a shade less painfully, he thought, than in the days before. He went to his basin. The looking-glass showed him a face which still looked alarmingly old and ill. He shaved, brushed his hair, took his grey pill, returned to bed with a book, and at once fell into a doze.

The ship's hooter roused him. That must be twelve noon. A knock on his door, barely audible above the other sea noises, and the dark face of his steward appeared.

'No good today,' the man said. 'Plenty passengers sick.'

He took the cup of tea and slipped away.

Mr Pinfold was a good sailor. Only once in a war which had been largely spent bucketing about in various sorts of boat, had he ever been seasick, and on that occasion most of the naval crew had been prostrate also. Mr Pinfold, who was neither beautiful nor athletic, cherished this one gift of parsimonious Nature. He decided to get up.

The main deck, when he reached it, was almost deserted. Two wind-blown girls in thick sweaters were tacking along arm-in-arm past the piles of folded chairs. Mr Pinfold hobbled to the after smoking-room bar. Four or five men sat together in one corner. He nodded to them, found a chair on the further side, and ordered brandy and ginger-ale. He was not himself. He knew in a distant way, as he knew, or thought he knew, certain facts of history, that he was in a ship, travelling for the good of his health, but, as with much of his historical knowledge, he was vague about the date. He did not know that twenty-four hours ago he had been in the train from London to Liverpool. His phases of sleeping and waking in the last few days were not related to night and day. He sat still in the smoking-room gazing blankly ahead.

After a time two cheerful women entered. The men greeted them:

'Morning, Mrs Cockson. Glad to see you're on your feet this merry morning.'

'Good morning, good morning, good morning all. You know Mrs Benson?'

'I don't think I've had that pleasure. Will you join us, Mrs Benson? I'm in the chair,' and he turned and called to the steward: 'Boy.'

Mr Pinfold studied this group with benevolence. No one among them would be a Pinfold fan. Presently, at one o'clock, a steward appeared with a gong and Mr Pinfold followed him submissively down to the dining-saloon.

The Captain's table was laid for seven. The 'fiddles' were up and the cloth damped; barely a quarter of the places in the saloon were taken.

Only one other of the Captain's party came to luncheon, a tall young Englishman who fell into easy conversation with Mr Pinfold, informing him that he was named

Glover and was manager of a tea plantation in Ceylon; an idyllic life, as he described it, lived on horseback with frequent long leave at a golf club. Glover was keen on golf. In order to keep himself in condition for the game on board ship he had a weighted club, its head on a spring, which he swung, he said, a hundred times morning and evening. His cabin, it transpired, was next to Mr Pinfold's.

'We have to share a bathroom. When do you like your bath?'

Glover's conversation did not demand sharp attention. Mr Pinfold found himself recalled into a world beyond which he had momentarily wandered, to answer: 'Well, really, I hardly ever have a bath at sea. One keeps so clean and I don't like hot salt water. I tried to book a private bathroom. I can't think why.'

'There aren't any private baths in this ship.'

'So I learned. It seems a very decent sort of ship,' said Mr Pinfold, gazing sadly at his curry, at his swaying glass of wine, at the surrounding deserted table, wishing to be pleasant to Glover.

'Yes. Everyone knows everyone else. The same people travel in her every year. People sometimes complain they feel rather out of things if they aren't regulars.'

'I shan't complain,' said Mr Pinfold. 'I've been rather ill. I want a quiet time.'

'Sorry to hear that. You'll find it quiet enough. Some find it too quiet.'

'It can't be too quiet for me,' said Mr Pinfold.

He took rather formal leave of Glover and at once forgot him until, reaching his cabin, he found added to its other noises the strains of a jazz band. Mr Pinfold stood puzzled. He was not musical. All he knew was that somewhere quite near him a band was playing. Then he remembered.

'It's the golfer,' he thought. 'That young man next door. He's got a gramophone. What's more,' he suddenly observed, 'he's got a *dog*.' Quite distinctly on the linoleum outside his door, between his door and Glover's, he heard the pattering of a dog's feet. 'I bet he's not allowed it. I've never been in a ship where they allowed dogs in the cabins. I daresay he bribed the steward. Anyway, one can't reasonably object. I don't mind. He seemed a very pleasant fellow.'

He noticed his grey pills, took one, lay down, opened his book, and then to the sound of dance tunes and the snuffling of the dog he fell asleep once more.

Perhaps he dreamed. He forgot on the instant whatever had happened in the hours between. It was dark. He was awake and there was a very curious scene being played near him; under his feet, it seemed. He heard distinctly a clergyman conducting a religious meeting. Mr Pinfold had no first-hand acquaintance with evangelical practice. His home and his schools had professed a broad-to-high anglicanism. His ideas of nonconformity derived from literature, from Mr Chadband and Philip Henry Gosse, from charades and from back numbers of *Punch*. The sermon, which was just rising to its peroration, was plainly an expression of that kind of faith, scriptural in diction, emotional in appeal. It was addressed presumably to members of the crew. Male voices sang a hymn which Mr Pinfold remembered from his nursery where his nanny, like almost all nannies, had been Calvinist: '*Pull for the shore, sailor. Pull for the shore.*'

'I want to see Billy alone after you dismiss,' said the clergyman. There followed an extempore, rather perfunctory prayer, then a great shuffling of feet and pushing about of chairs; then a hush; then the clergyman, very earnestly: 'Well, Billy, what have you got to say to me?' and the unmistakable sound of sobbing.

Mr Pinfold began to feel uneasy. This was something that was not meant to be overheard.

'Billy, you must tell me yourself. I am not accusing you of anything. I am not putting words into your mouth.'

Silence except for sobbing.

'Billy, you know what we talked about last time. Have you done it again? Have you been impure, Billy?'

'Yes, sir. I can't help it, sir.'

'God never tempts us beyond our strength, Billy. I've told you that, haven't I? Do you suppose I do not feel these temptations, too, Billy? Very strongly at times. But I resist, don't I? You know I resist, don't I, Billy?'

Mr Pinfold was horror-struck. He was being drawn into participation in a scene of gruesome indecency. His sticks lay by the bunk. He took the blackthorn and beat strongly on the floor.

'Did you hear anything then, Billy? A knocking. That is God knocking at the door of your soul. He can't come and help you unless you are pure, like me.'

This was more than Mr Pinfold could bear. He took painfully to his feet, put on his coat, brushed his hair. The voices below him continued:

'I can't help it, sir. I want to be good. I try. I can't.'

'You've got pictures of girls stuck up by your bunk, haven't you?'

'Yes, sir.'

'Filthy pictures.'

'Yes, sir.'

'How can you say you want to be good when you keep temptation deliberately before your eyes. I shall come and destroy those pictures.'

'No, please, sir. I want them.'

Mr Pinfold hobbled out of his cabin and up to the main

deck. The sea was calmer now. More passengers were about in the lounge and the bar. It was half past six. A group were throwing dice for drinks. Mr Pinfold sat alone and ordered a cocktail. When the steward brought it, he asked: 'Does this ship carry a regular chaplain?'

'Oh no, sir. The Captain reads the prayers on Sundays.'

'There's a clergyman, then, among the passengers?'

'I haven't seen one, sir. Here's the list.'

Mr Pinfold studied the passenger list. No name bore any prefix indicating Holy Orders. A strange ship, thought Mr Pinfold, in which laymen were allowed to evangelize a presumably heathen crew; religious mania perhaps on the part of one of the officers.

Waking and sleeping he had lost count of time. It seemed he had been many days at sea in this strange ship. When Glover came into the bar, Mr Pinfold said affably: 'Nice to see you again.'

Glover looked slightly startled by this greeting.

'I've been down in my cabin,' he said.

'I had to come up. I was embarrassed by that prayer-meeting. Weren't you?'

'Prayer-meeting?' said Glover. 'No.'

'Right under our feet. Couldn't you hear it?'

'I heard nothing,' said Glover.

He began to move away.

'Have a drink,' said Mr Pinfold.

'I won't thanks. I don't. Have to be careful in a place like Ceylon.'

'How's your dog?'

'My dog?'

'Your crypto-dog. The stowaway. Please don't think I'm complaining. I don't mind your dog. Nor your gramophone for that matter.'

'But I haven't a dog. I haven't a gramophone.'

'Oh well,' said Mr Pinfold huffily. 'Perhaps I am mistaken.'

If Glover did not wish to confide in him, he would not try to force himself on the young man.

'See you at dinner,' said Glover, making off.

He was wearing a dinner jacket, Mr Pinfold noticed, as were several other passengers. Time to change. Mr Pinfold went back to his cabin. No sound came now from below; the pseudo-priest and the unchaste seaman had left. But the jazz band was going full blast. So it was not Glover's gramophone. As he changed, Mr Pinfold considered the matter. During the war he had travelled in troopships which were fitted with amplifiers on every deck. Unintelligible alarms and orders had issued from these devices and at certain hours popular music. The *Caliban*, plainly, was equipped in this way. It would be a great nuisance when he began to write. He would have to inquire whether there was some way of cutting it off.

It took him a long time to dress. His fingers were unusually clumsy with studs and tie, and his face in the glass was still blotched and staring. By the time he was ready the gong was sounding for dinner. He did not attempt to wear his evening shoes. Instead he slipped into the soft, fur-lined boots in which he had come aboard. With one hand firmly on the rail, the other on his cane, he made his way laboriously down to the saloon. On the stairs he noticed a bronze plaque recording that this ship had been manned by the Royal Navy during the war and had served in the landing in North Africa and Normandy.

He was first at his table, one of the earliest diners in the ship. He noticed a small dark man in day clothes sitting at a table alone. Then the place began to fill. He watched his fellow passengers in a slightly dazed way. The purser's table, as is common in ships of the kind, had the gayest party, the

few girls and young women, the more jovial men from the
bar. A plate of soup was set before Mr Pinfold. Two or three
coloured stewards stood together by a service table talking
in undertones. Suddenly Mr Pinfold was surprised to hear
from them three obscene epithets spoken in clear English
tones. He looked and glared. One of the men immediately slid
to his side.

'Yes, sir; something to drink, sir?'

There was no hint of mockery in the gentle face, no echo
in that soft South Indian accent of the gross tones he had
overheard. Baffled, Mr Pinfold said: 'Wine.'

'Wine, sir?'

'You have some champagne on board, I suppose?'

'Oh yes, sir. Three names. I show list.'

'Don't bother about the name. Just bring half a bottle.'

Glover came and sat opposite.

'I owe you an apology,' said Mr Pinfold. 'It wasn't your
gramophone. Part of the naval equipment left over from the
war.'

'Oh,' said Glover. 'That was it, was it?'

'It seems the most likely explanation.'

'Perhaps it does.'

'Very odd language the servants use.'

'They're from Travancore.'

'No. I mean the way they swear. In front of us, I mean.
I daresay they don't mean to be insolent but it shows bad
discipline.'

'I've never noticed it,' said Glover.

He was not at his ease with Mr Pinfold.

Then the table filled up. Captain Steerforth greeted them
and took his place at the head. He was an unremarkable man
at first sight. A pretty, youngish woman introduced as Mrs
Scarfield sat next to Mr Pinfold. He explained that he was

temporarily a cripple and could not stand up. 'My doctor has given me some awfully strong pills to take. They make me feel rather odd. You must forgive me if I'm a dull companion.'

'We're all very dull, I'm afraid,' she said. 'You're the writer, aren't you? I'm afraid I never seem to get any time for reading.'

Mr Pinfold was inured to this sort of conversation but tonight he could not cope. He said: 'I wish I didn't', and turned stupidly to his wine. 'She probably thinks I'm drunk,' he thought and made an attempt to explain: 'They are big grey pills. I don't know what's in them. I don't believe my doctor does either. Something new.'

'That's always exciting, isn't it?' said Mrs Scarfield.

Mr Pinfold despaired and spent the rest of dinner, at which he ate very little, in silence.

The Captain rose, his party with him. Mr Pinfold, slow to move, was still in his chair, fumbling for his stick, when they passed behind him. He got to his feet. He would have dearly liked to go to his cabin, but he was held back, partly by the odd fear that he would be suspected of sea-sickness but more by an odder sentiment, a bond of duty which he conceived held him to Captain Steerforth. It seemed to him that he was in some way under this man's command and that it would be a grave default to leave him until he was dismissed. So, laboriously, he followed them to the lounge and lowered himself into an armchair between the Scarfields. They were drinking coffee. He offered them all brandy. They refused and for himself he ordered brandy and crème de menthe mixed. As he did so Mr and Mrs Scarfield exchanged a glance, which he intercepted, as though to confirm some previous confidence – 'My dear, that man next to me, the author, was completely tight.' 'Are you sure?' 'Simply plastered.'

Mrs Scarfield was really extremely pretty, Mr Pinfold thought. She would not keep that skin long in Burma.

Mr Scarfield was in the timber trade, teak. His prospects depended less on his own industry and acumen than on the action of politicians. He addressed the little circle on this subject.

'In a democracy,' said Mr Pinfold with more weight than originality, 'men do not seek authority so that they may impose a policy. They seek a policy so that they may achieve authority.'

He proceeded to illustrate this theme with examples.

At one time or another he had met most of the Government Front Bench. Some were members of Bellamy's whom he knew well. Oblivious of his audience he began to speak of them with familiarity, as he would have done among his friends. The Scarfields again exchanged glances and it occurred to him, too late, that he was not among people who thought it on the whole rather discreditable to know politicians. These people thought he was showing off. He stopped in the middle of a sentence, silent with shame.

'It must be very exciting to move behind the scenes,' said Mrs Scarfield. 'We only know what we see in the papers.'

Was there malice behind her smile? At first meeting she had seemed frank and friendly. Mr Pinfold thought he discovered sly hostility now.

'Oh, I hardly ever read the political columns,' he said.

'You don't have to, do you? getting it all first hand.'

There was no doubt in Mr Pinfold's mind. He had made an ass of himself. Reckless now of his reputation as a good sailor, he attempted a little bow to include the Captain and the Scarfields.

'If you'll excuse me, I think I'll go to my cabin.'

He had difficulty getting out of his deep chair, he had difficulty with his stick, he had difficulty keeping his balance.

They had barely said 'Good night', he was still struggling away from them, when something the Captain said made them laugh. Three distinct laughs, all, in Mr Pinfold's ears, cruelly derisive. On his way out he passed Glover. Moved to explain himself he said: 'I don't know anything about politics.'

'No?' said Glover.

'Tell them I don't know anything.'

'Tell who?'

'The Captain.'

'He's just behind you over there.'

'Oh well, it doesn't matter.'

He hobbled away and looking back from the doors saw Glover talking to the Scarfields. They were ostensibly arranging a four for bridge but Mr Pinfold knew they had another darker interest – *him*.

It was not yet nine o'clock. Mr Pinfold undressed. He hung up his clothes, washed, and took his pill. There were three tablespoonfuls left in his bottle of sleeping-draught. He decided to try and spend the night without it, to delay anyway until after midnight. The sea was much calmer now; he could lie in bed without rolling. He lay at ease and began to read one of the novels he had brought on board.

Then, before he had turned a page, the band struck up. This was no wireless performance. It was a living group just under his feet, rehearsing. They were in the same place, as inexplicably audible, as the afternoon bible-class; young happy people, the party doubtless from the purser's table. Their instruments were drums and rattles and some sort of pipe. The drums and rattles did most of the work. Mr Pinfold knew nothing of music. It seemed to him that the rhythms they played derived from some very primitive tribe and were of anthropological rather than artistic interest. This guess was confirmed.

'Let's try the Pocoputa Indian one,' said the young man who acted, without any great air of authority, as leader.

'Oh not *that*. It's so *beastly*,' said a girl.

'I know,' said the leader. 'It's the three-eight rhythm. The Gestapo discovered it independently, you know. They used to play it in the cells. It drove the prisoners mad.'

'Yes,' said another girl. 'Thirty-six hours did for anyone. Twelve was enough for most. They could stand any torture but that.'

'It drove them absolutely mad.' 'Raving mad.' 'Stark, staring mad.' 'It was the worst torture of all.' 'The Russians use it now.' The voices, some male, some female, all young and eager, came tumbling like puppies. 'The Hungarians do it best.' 'Good old three-eight.' 'Good old Pocoputa Indians.' 'They were mad.'

'I suppose no one can hear us?' said a sweet girlish voice.

'Don't be so wet, Mimi. Everyone's up on the main deck.'

'All right then,' said the band leader. 'The three-eight rhythm.'

And off they went.

The sound throbbed and thrilled in the cabin which had suddenly become a prison cell. Mr Pinfold was not one who thought and talked easily to a musical accompaniment. Even in early youth he had sought the night-clubs where there was a bar out of hearing of the band. Friends he had, Roger Stillingfleet among them, to whom jazz was a necessary drug – whether stimulant or narcotic Mr Pinfold did not know. He preferred silence. The three-eight rhythm was indeed torture to him. He could not read. It was not a quarter of an hour since he had entered the cabin. Unendurable hours lay ahead. He emptied the bottle of sleeping-draught and, to the strains of the jolly young people from the purser's table, fell into unconsciousness.

He awoke before dawn. The bright young people below him had dispersed. The three-eight rhythm was hushed. No shadow passed between the deck-light and the cabin-window. But overhead there was turmoil. The crew, or a considerable part of it, was engaged on an operation of dragging the deck with what from the sound of it might have been an enormous chain-harrow, and they were not happy in their work. They were protesting mutinously in their own tongue and the officer in command was roaring back at them in the tones of an old sea-dog: 'Get on with it, you black bastards. Get on with it.'

The lascars were not so easily quelled. They shouted back unintelligibly.

'I'll call out the Master-at-Arms,' shouted the officer. An empty threat, surely? thought Mr Pinfold. It was scarcely conceivable that the *Caliban* carried a Master-at-Arms. 'By God, I'll shoot the first man of you that moves,' said the officer.

The hubbub increased. Mr Pinfold could almost see the drama overhead, the half-lighted deck, the dark frenzied faces, the solitary bully with the heavy old-fashioned ship's pistol. Then there was a crash, not a shot but a huge percussion of metal as though a hundred pokers and pairs of tongs had fallen into an enormous fender, followed by a wail of agony and a moment of complete silence.

'There,' said the officer more in the tones of a nanny than a sea-dog, 'just see what you've gone and done now.'

Whatever its nature this violent occurrence entirely subdued the passions of the crew. They were docile, ready to do anything to retrieve the disaster. The only sounds now were the officer's calmer orders and the whimpering of the injured man.

'Steady there. Easy does it. You, cut along to the sick-bay and get the surgeon. You, go up and report to the bridge . . .'

For a long time, two hours perhaps, Mr Pinfold lay in his
bunk listening. He was able to hear quite distinctly not only
what was said in his immediate vicinity, but elsewhere. He
had the light on, now, in his cabin, and as he gazed at the complex of tubes and wires which ran across his ceiling, he realized
that they must form some kind of general junction in the
system of communication. Through some trick or fault or
wartime survival everything spoken in the executive quarters
of the ship was transmitted to him. A survival seemed the
most likely explanation. Once during the blitz in London he
had been given a hotel bedroom which had been hastily
vacated by a visiting allied statesman. When he lifted the
telephone to order his breakfast, he had found himself talking
on a private line direct to the Cabinet Office. Something of
that kind must have happened in the *Caliban*. When she was a
naval vessel this cabin had no doubt been the office of some
operational headquarters and when she was handed back to
her owners and re-adapted for passenger service, the engineers
had neglected to disconnect it. That alone could explain the
voices which now kept him informed of every stage of the
incident.

The wounded man seemed to have got himself entangled
in some kind of web of metal. Various unsuccessful and
agonizing attempts were made to extricate him. Finally the
decision was taken to cut him out. The order once given was
carried out with surprising speed but the contraption, whatever it was, was ruined in the process and was finally dragged
across the deck and thrown overboard. The victim continuously sobbed and whimpered. He was taken to the sick-bay
and put in charge of a kind but not, it appeared, very highly
qualified nurse. 'You must be brave,' she said. 'I will say the
rosary for you. You must be brave,' while the wireless tele-
graphist got into touch with a hospital ashore and was given

instructions in first-aid. The ship's surgeon never appeared. Details of treatment were dictated from the shore and passed to the sick-bay. The last words Mr Pinfold heard from the bridge were Captain Steerforth's 'I'm not going to be bothered with a sick man on board. We'll have to signal a passing homebound ship and have him transferred.'

Part of the treatment prescribed by the hospital was a sedative injection, and as this spread its relief over the unhappy lascar, Mr Pinfold too grew drowsy until finally he fell asleep to the sound of the nurse murmuring the Angelic Salutation.

He was awakened by the coloured cabin steward bringing him tea.

'Very disagreeable business that last night,' said Mr Pinfold.

'Yes, sir.'

'How is the poor fellow?'

'Eight o'clock, sir.'

'Have they managed to get into touch with a ship to take him off?'

'Yes, sir. Breakfast eight-thirty, sir.'

Mr Pinfold drank his tea. He felt disinclined to get up. The intercommunication system was silent. He picked up his book and began to read. Then with a click the voices began again.

Captain Steerforth seemed to be addressing a deputation of the crew. 'I want you to understand,' he was saying, 'that a great quantity of valuable metal was sacrificed last night for the welfare of a single seaman. That metal was pure *copper*. One of the most valuable metals in the world. Mind you I don't regret the sacrifice and I am sure the Company will approve my action. But I want you all to appreciate that only in a British ship would such a thing be done. In the ship of any other nationality it would have been the seaman not the metal that was cut up. You know that as well as I do. Don't forget it.

And another thing, instead of taking the man with us to Port Said and the filth of a Wog hospital, I had him carefully trans-shipped and he is now on his way to England. He couldn't have been treated more handsomely if he'd been a director of the Company. I know the hospital he's going to; it's a sweet, pretty place. It's the place all seamen long to go to. He'll have the best attention there and live, if he does live, in the greatest comfort. That's the kind of ship this is. Nothing is too good for the men who serve in her.'

The meeting seemed to disperse. There was a shuffling and muttering and presently a woman spoke. It was a voice which was soon to become familiar to Mr Pinfold. To all men and women there is some sound – grating, perhaps, or rustling, or strident, deep or shrill, a note or inflection of speech – which causes peculiar pain; which literally 'makes the hair stand on end' or metaphorically 'sets the teeth on edge'; something which Dr Drake would have called an 'allergy'. Such was this woman's voice. It clearly did not affect the Captain in this way but to Mr Pinfold it was excruciating.

'Well,' said this voice. 'That should teach them not to grumble.'

'Yes,' said Captain Steerforth. 'We've settled that little mutiny, I think. We shouldn't have any trouble now.'

'Not till the next time,' said the cynical woman. 'What a contemptible exhibition that man made of himself – crying like a child. Thank God we've seen the last of him. I liked your touch about the sweet, pretty hospital.'

'Yes. They little know the Hell-spot I've sent him to. Spoiling my copper, indeed. He'll soon wish he were in Port Said.'

And the woman laughed odiously. 'Soon wish he was dead,' she said.

There was a click (someone seemed to be in control of the apparatus, Mr Pinfold thought), and two passengers were speaking. They seemed to be elderly, military gentlemen.

'I think the passengers should be told,' one said.

'Yes, we ought to call a meeting. It's the sort of thing that so often passes without proper recognition. We ought to pass a vote of thanks.'

'A ton of copper, you say?'

'Pure copper, cut up and chucked overboard. All for the sake of a nigger. It makes one proud of the British service.'

The voices ceased and Mr Pinfold lay wondering about this meeting; was it his duty to attend and report what he knew of the true characters of the Captain and his female associate? The difficulty, of course, would be to prove his charges; to explain satisfactorily, how he came to overhear the Captain's secret.

Soft music filled the cabin, an oratorio sung by a great but distant choir. 'That *must* be a gramophone record,' thought Mr Pinfold. 'Or the wireless. They can't be performing this on board.' Then he slept for some time, until he was woken by a change of music. The bright young people were at it again with their Pocoputa Indian three-eight rhythm. Mr Pinfold looked at his watch. Eleven-thirty. Time to get up.

As he laboriously shaved and dressed, he reasoned closely about his situation. Now that he knew of the intercommunication system, it was plain to him that the room used by this band might be anywhere in the ship. The prayer-meeting too. It had seemed odd at the time that the quiet voices had come so clearly through the floor; that they had been audible to him and not to Glover. That was now explained. But he was puzzled by the irregularity, by the changes of place, the clicking on and off. It was improbable that anyone at a switchboard was directing the annoyances into his cabin. It was certain that the Captain would not deliberately broadcast his private and compromising conversations. Mr Pinfold wished he knew more of the mechanics of the thing. He remembered that in London just after the war, when everything was worn out, telephones used sometimes to behave in this erratic way; the line would go dead; then crackle; then, when the tangled wire was given a twist and a jerk, normal conversation was rejoined. He supposed that somewhere over his head, in the ventilation shaft probably, there were a number of frayed and partly disconnected wires which every now and then with the movement of the ship came into contact and so established communication now with one, now with another part of the ship.

Before leaving his cabin he considered his box of pills. He was not well. Much was wrong with him, he felt, beside lameness. Dr Drake did not know about the sleeping-draught. It might be that the pills, admittedly new and pretty strong, warred with the bromide and chloral; perhaps with gin and brandy too. Well, the sleeping-draught was finished. He would try the pills once or twice more. He swallowed one and crept up to the main deck.

Here there was light and liveliness, a glitter of cool sunshine and a brisk breeze. The young people had abandoned the concert in the short time it had taken Mr Pinfold to climb the stairs. They were on the after deck playing quoits and shuffle-board and watching one another play; laughing boisterously as the ship rolled and jostled them against one another. Mr Pinfold leant on the rail and looked down, thinking it odd that such healthy-seeming, good-natured creatures should rejoice in the music of the Pocoputa Indians. Glover stood by himself in the stern swinging his golf-club. On the sunny side of the main deck the older passengers sat wrapped in rugs, some with popular biographies, some with knitting.

The young Burmese paced together in pairs, uniformly and neatly dressed in blazers and pale fawn trousers, like officers waiting to fall in at a battalion parade.

Mr Pinfold sought the military gentlemen whose ill-informed eulogies of the Captain he believed it to be his duty to correct. From the voices, elderly, precise, conventional, he had formed a clear idea of their appearance. They were major-generals, retired now. They had been gallant young regimental officers – line-cavalry probably – in 1914 and had commanded brigades at the end of that war. They had passed at the Staff College and waited patiently for another battle only to find in 1939 that they were passed over for active command. But they had served loyally in offices, done their turn at fire-watching, gone short of whisky and razor-blades. Now they could just afford an inexpensive winter cruise every other year; admirable old men in their way. He did not find them on deck or in any of the public rooms.

As noon was sounded there was a movement towards the bar for the announcement of the ship's run and the result of the sweepstake. Scarfield was the winner of a modest prize. He ordered drinks for all in sight including Mr Pinfold. Mrs Scarfield stood near him and Mr Pinfold said: 'I say, I'm afraid I was an awful bore last night.'

'Were you?' she said. 'Not while you were with us.'

'All that nonsense I talked about politics. It's those pills I have to take. They make me feel rather odd.'

'I'm sorry about that,' said Mrs Scarfield, 'but I assure you, you didn't bore *us* in the least. I was fascinated.'

Mr Pinfold looked hard at her but could detect no hint of irony. 'Anyway I shan't hold forth like that again.'

'Please do.'

The ladies who had been identified as Mrs Benson and Mrs Cockson were in the same chairs as on the day before. They liked their glass, that pair, thought Mr Pinfold with approval; good sorts. He greeted them. He greeted anyone who caught his eye. He was feeling very much better.

One figure alone remained aloof from the general conviviality, the dark little man whom Mr Pinfold had noticed dining alone.

Presently the steward passed by, tapping his little musical gong, and Mr Pinfold followed the company down to luncheon. Knowing what he did of Captain Steerforth's character, Mr Pinfold found it rather repugnant to sit at the table with him. He gave him a perfunctory nod and addressed himself to Glover.

'Noisy night, wasn't it?'

'Oh,' said Glover, 'I didn't hear anything.'

'You must sleep very sound.'

'As a matter of fact, I didn't. I usually do, but I am not getting the exercise I'm used to. I was awake half the night.'

'And you didn't hear the accident?'

'No.'

'Accident?' said Mrs Scarfield overhearing. 'Was there an accident last night, Captain?'

'No one told me of one,' said Captain Steerforth blandly.

'The villain,' thought Mr Pinfold. 'Remorseless, treacherous, lecherous, kindless villain,' for though Captain Steerforth had shown no other symptoms of lechery, Mr Pinfold knew instinctively that his relations with the harsh-voiced woman – stewardess, secretary, passenger, whatever she might be – were grossly erotic.

'What accident, Mr Pinfold?' asked Mrs Scarfield.

'Perhaps I was mistaken,' said Mr Pinfold stiffly. 'I often am.'

There was another couple at the Captain's table. They had been there the night before, had been part of the group in which Mr Pinfold had talked so injudiciously, but he had barely noticed them; a pleasant, middle-aged nondescript, rather rich-looking couple, not English, Dutch perhaps or Scandinavian. The woman now leant across and said in thick, rather arch tones:

'There are two books of yours in the ship's library, I find.'

'Ah.'

'I have taken one. It is named *The Last Card*.'

'*The Lost Chord*,' said Mr Pinfold.

'Yes. It is a humorous book, yes?'

'Some people have suggested as much.'

'I find it so. It is not your suggestion also? I think you have a peculiar sense of humour, Mr Pinfold.'

'Ah.'

'That is what you are known for, yes, your peculiar sense of humour?'

'Perhaps.'

'May I have it after you?' asked Mrs Scarfield. 'Everyone says I have a peculiar sense of humour too.'

'But not so peculiar as Mr Pinfold?'

'That remains to be seen,' said Mrs Scarfield.

'I think you're embarrassing the author,' said Mr Scarfield.

'I expect he's used to it,' she said.

'He takes it all with his peculiar sense of humour,' said the foreign lady.

'If you'll excuse me,' said Mr Pinfold, struggling to rise.

'You see he is embarrassed.'

'No,' said the foreign lady. 'It is his humour. He is going to make notes of us. You see, we shall all be in a humorous book.'

As Mr Pinfold rose, he gazed towards the little dark man at his solitary table. That is where he should have been, he

thought. The last sound he heard as he left the dining-saloon
was merry young laughter from the purser's table.

Since he left it, not much more than an hour before, the
cabin had been tidied and the bedclothes stretched taut,
hospital-like, across the bunk. He took off his coat and his soft
boots, lit a cigar, and lay down. He had barely eaten at all that
day but he was not hungry. He blew smoke up towards the
wires and pipes on the ceiling and wondered how without
offence he could escape from the Captain's table to sit and
eat alone, silent and untroubled, like that clever, dark, enviable
little fellow, and as though in response to these thoughts the
device overhead clicked into life and he heard this very
subject being debated by the two old soldiers.

'My dear fellow, *I* don't care a damn.'

'No, of course you don't. Nor do I. All the same I think
it very decent of him to mention it.'

'*Very* decent. What did he say exactly?'

'Said he was very sorry he hadn't room for you and me
and my missus. The table only takes six passengers. Well,
he had to have the Scarfields.'

'Yes, of course. He *had* to have the Scarfields.'

'Yes, he had to have them. Then there's the Norwegian
couple – foreigners you know.'

'Distinguished foreigners.'

'Got to be civil to them. Well that makes four. Then if
you please, he got an order from the Company to take this
fellow Pinfold. So he only had one place. Knew he couldn't
separate you and me and the missus, so he asked that decent
young fellow – the one with the uncle in Liverpool.'

'Has he got an uncle in Liverpool?'

'Yes, yes. That's why he asked him.'

'But why did he ask Pinfold?'

'Company's orders. *He* didn't want him.'

'No, no, of course not.'

'If you ask me Pinfold drinks.'

'Yes, so I have always heard.'

'I saw him come on board. He was tight then. In a beastly state.'

'He's been in a beastly state ever since.'

'He says it's pills.'

'No, no, drink. I've seen better men than Pinfold go that way.'

'Wretched business. He shouldn't have come.'

'If you ask me he's been *sent* on this ship as a *cure*.'

'Ought to have someone to look after him.'

'Have you noticed that little dark chap who sits alone? I shouldn't be surprised if *he* wasn't keeping an eye on him.'

'A male nurse?'

'A warder more likely.'

'Put on him by his missus without his knowing?'

'That's my appreciation of the situation.'

The voices of the two old gossips faded and fell silent. Mr Pinfold lay smoking, without resentment. It was the sort of thing one expected to have said behind one's back – the sort of thing one said about other people. It was slightly unnerving to overhear it. The idea of his wife setting a spy on him was amusing. He would write and tell her. The question of his drunkenness interested him more. Perhaps he did give that impression. Perhaps on that first evening at sea – how long ago was that now? – when he had talked politics after dinner, perhaps he *had* drunk too much. He had had too much of something certainly, pills or sleeping-draught or liquor. Well, the sleeping-draught was finished. He resolved to take no more pills. He would stick to wine and a cocktail or two and a glass of brandy after dinner and soon he would be well and active once more.

He had reached the last inch of his cigar, a large one, an hour's smoking, when his reverie was interrupted from the Captain's cabin.

The doxy was there. In her harsh voice she said: 'You've got to teach him a lesson.'

'I will.'

'A *good* lesson.'

'Yes.'

'One he won't forget.'

'Bring him in.'

There was a sound of scuffling and whimpering, a sound rather like that of the wounded seaman whom Mr Pinfold had heard that morning; which morning? One morning of this disturbing voyage. It seemed that a prisoner was being dragged into the Captain's presence.

'Tie him to the chair,' said the leman, and Mr Pinfold at once thought of *King Lear*: 'Bind fast his corky arms.' Who said that? Goneril? Regan? Perhaps neither of them. Cornwall? It was a man's voice, surely? in the play. But it was the voice of the woman, or what passed as a woman, here. Addict of nicknames as he was, Mr Pinfold there and then dubbed her 'Goneril'.

'All right,' said Captain Steerforth, 'you can leave him to me.'

'And to me,' said Goneril.

Mr Pinfold was not abnormally squeamish nor had his life been particularly sheltered, but he had no experience of personal, physical cruelty and no liking for its portrayal in books or films. Now, lying in his spruce cabin in this British ship, in the early afternoon, a few yards distance from Glover and the Scarfields, Mrs Benson and Mrs Cockson, he was the horrified witness of a scene which might have come straight from the kind of pseudo-American thriller he most abhorred.

There were three people in the Captain's cabin, Steerforth, Goneril, and their prisoner, who was one of the coloured stewards. Proceedings began with a form of trial. Goneril gave her evidence, vindictively but precisely accusing the man of an attempted sexual offence against her. It sounded to Mr Pinfold rather a strong case. Knowing the ambiguous position which the accuser held in the ship, remembering the gross language he had overheard in the dining-saloon and the heavy, unhealthy discourse of the preacher, Mr Pinfold considered the incident he heard described exactly the sort of thing he would expect to happen in this beastly ship. Guilty, he thought.

'Guilty,' said the Captain and at the word Goneril vented a hiss of satisfaction and anticipation. Slowly and deliberately, as the ship steamed South with its commonplace load of passengers, the Captain and his leman with undisguised erotic enjoyment settled down to torture their prisoner.

Mr Pinfold could not surmise what form the torture took. He could only listen to the moans and sobs of the victim and the more horrific, ecstatic, orgiastic cries of Goneril:

'More. More. Again. Again. Again. You haven't had anything yet, you beast. Give him some more, more, more, more.'

Mr Pinfold could not endure it. He must stop this outrage at once. He lurched from his bunk, but even as he felt for his boots, silence fell in the Captain's cabin and a suddenly sobered Goneril said: 'That's enough.'

Not a sound came from the victim. After a long pause Captain Steerforth said: 'If you ask me, it's too much.'

'He's shamming,' said Goneril without conviction.

'He's dead,' said the Captain.

'Well,' said Goneril. 'What are you going to do about it?'

'Untie him.'

'I'm not going to touch him. I never touched him. It was all *you*.'

Mr Pinfold stood in his cabin, just as, no doubt, the Captain was standing in his, uncertain what to do, and as he hesitated, he realized through his horror that the pains in his legs had suddenly entirely ceased. He rose on his toes; he bent his knees. He was cured. It was the way in which these attacks of his always came and went, quite unpredictably. In spite of his agitation he had room in his mind to consider whether perhaps they were nervous in origin, whether the shock he had just endured might not have succeeded where the grey pills had failed; whether he had not been healed by the steward's agony. It was a hypothesis which momentarily distracted him from the murderer above.

Presently he turned to listen to them.

'As master of the ship I shall make out a death-certificate and have him put overboard after dark.'

'How about the surgeon?'

'He must sign too. The first thing is to get the body into the sick-bay. We don't want any more trouble with the men. Get Margaret.'

The situation as Mr Pinfold saw it was appalling but it did not call for action.

Whatever had to be done need not be done now. He could not burst alone into the Captain's cabin and denounce him. What was the proper procedure, if any existed, for putting a Captain in irons in his own ship? He would have to take advice. The military men, that sage, authoritative couple, were the obvious people. He would find them and explain the situation. They would know what to do. A report must be made, he assumed, depositions taken. Where? At the first consulate they came to, at Port Said; or should they wait until they reached a British port? Those old campaigners would know.

Meanwhile Margaret, the kind nurse, a sort of Cordelia, seemed to have charge of the body. 'Poor boy, poor boy,' she was saying. 'Look at these ghastly marks. You can't say these are "natural causes".'

'That's what the Captain says,' said a new voice, the ship's surgeon presumably. 'I take my orders from him. There's a lot goes on aboard this ship that I don't like. The best you can do, young lady, is to see nothing, hear nothing, and say nothing.'

'But the poor boy. He must have suffered so.'

'Natural causes,' said the doctor. And then there was silence.

Mr Pinfold removed his soft boots and put on shoes. He propped his two sticks in a corner of the wardrobe. 'I shan't need those again,' he reflected, little knowing what the coming days had in store, and walked almost blithely to the main deck.

No one was about except two lascars, slung overhead, painting the davits. It was half past three, a time when all the passengers were in their cabins. Like a lark on a battlefield Mr Pinfold's spirits rose, free and singing. He rejoiced in his power to walk. He walked round the ship, again and again, up and down. Was it possible, in this bright and peaceful scene, to believe in the abomination that lurked up there, just overhead, behind the sparkling paint? Could he possibly be mistaken? He had never seen Goneril. He barely knew the Captain's voice. Could he really identify it? Was it not possible that what he had heard was a piece of acting – a charade of the bright young peoples? a broadcast from London?

Wishful thinking, perhaps, born on the exhilaration of sun and sea and wind and his own newfound health?

Time alone would show.

4

THE HOOLIGANS

That evening Mr Pinfold felt the renewal of health and cheerfulness and clarity of mind greater, it seemed to him, than he had known for weeks. He looked at his hands, which for days now had been blotched with crimson; now they were clear and his face in the glass had lost its congested, mottled hue. He dressed more deftly and as he dressed the wireless in his cabin came into action.

'This is the B.B.C. Third Programme. Here is Mr Clutton-Cornforth to speak on Aspects of Orthodoxy in Contemporary Letters.'

Mr Pinfold had known Clutton-Cornforth for thirty years. He was now the editor of a literary weekly, an ambitious, obsequious fellow. Mr Pinfold had no curiosity about his opinions on any subject. He wished there were a way of switching off the fluting, fruity voice. He tried instead to disregard it until, just as he was leaving, he was recalled by the sound of his own name.

'Gilbert Pinfold,' he heard, 'poses a precisely antithetical problem, or should we say? the same problem in antithetical form. The basic qualities of a Pinfold novel seldom vary and may be enumerated thus: conventionality of plot, falseness of characterization, morbid sentimentality, gross and hackneyed farce alternating with grosser and more hackneyed melodrama; cloying religiosity, which will be found tedious or blasphemous according as the reader shares or repudiates his doctrinal preconceptions; an adventitious and offensive sensuality that is clearly introduced for commercial motives. All this is presented in a style which, when it varies from the trite, lapses into positive illiteracy.'

Really, thought Mr Pinfold, this was not like the Third Programme; it was not at all like Algernon Clutton-Cornforth. 'My word,' he thought, 'I'll give that booby such a kick on the sit-upon next time I see him waddling up the steps of the London Library.'

'Indeed,' continued Clutton-Cornforth, 'if one is asked – and one *is* often asked – to give one name which typifies all that is decadent in contemporary literature, one can answer without hesitation – Gilbert Pinfold. I now turn from him to the equally deplorable but more interesting case of a writer often associated with him – Roger Stillingfleet.'

Here, by a quirk of the apparatus, Clutton-Cornforth was cut off and succeeded by a female singer:

> '*I'm Gilbert, the filbert,*
> *The knut with the K,*
> *The pride of Piccadilly,*
> *The blasé roué.*'

Mr Pinfold left his cabin. He met the steward on his rounds with the dinner gong and ascended to the main-deck. He stepped out into the wind, leaned briefly on the rail, looked down into the surge of lighted water. The music rejoined him there, emanating from somewhere quite near where he stood.

> '*For Gilbert, the filbert,*
> *The Colonel of the Knuts.*'

Other people in the ship were listening to the wireless. Other people, probably, had heard Clutton-Cornforth's diatribe. Well, he was accustomed to criticism (though not

from Clutton-Cornforth). He could take it. He only hoped
no one bored him by talking about it; particularly not that
Norwegian woman at the Captain's table.

Mr Pinfold's feelings towards the Captain had moderated
in the course of the afternoon. As to whether the man were
guilty of murder or no, his judgement was suspended, but
the fact of his having fallen under a cloud, of Mr Pinfold's
possession of secret knowledge which might or might not
bring him to ruin, severed the bond of loyalty which had
previously bound them. Mr Pinfold felt disposed to tease the
Captain a little.

Accordingly at dinner, when they were all seated, and he
had ordered himself a pint of champagne, he turned the conversation rather abruptly to the subject of murder.

'Have you ever actually met a murderer?' he asked
Glover.

Glover had. In his tea garden a trusted foreman had hacked
his wife to pieces.

'I expect he smiled a good deal, didn't he?' asked Mr
Pinfold.

'Yes, as a matter of fact he did. Always a most cheerful
chap. He went off to be hanged laughing away with his
brothers as though it was no end of a joke.'

'*Exactly.*'

Mr Pinfold stared full in the eyes of the smiling Captain.
Was there any sign of alarm in that broad, plain face?

'Have *you* ever known a murderer, Captain Steerforth?'

Yes, when he first went to sea, Captain Steerforth had been
in a ship with a stoker who killed another with a shovel. But
they brought it in that the man was insane, affected by the heat
of the stokehold.

'In my country in the forests in the long winter often the
men become drunken and fight and sometimes they kill one

another. Is not hanging in my country for such things. Is a case for the doctor we think.'

'If you ask me all murderers are mad,' said Scarfield.

'And always smiling,' said Mr Pinfold. 'That's the only way you can tell them – by their inevitable good-humour.'

'This stoker wasn't very cheerful. Surly fellow as I remember him.'

'Ah, but he was mad.'

'Goodness,' said Mrs Scarfield, 'what a morbid subject. However did we get on to it?'

'Not so morbid by half as Clutton-Cornforth,' said Mr Pinfold rather truculently.

'Who?' asked Mrs Scarfield.

'As what?' asked the Norwegian woman.

Mr Pinfold looked from face to face round the table. Clearly no one had heard the broadcast.

'Oh,' he said, 'if you don't know about him, the less said the better.'

'Do tell,' said Mrs Scarfield.

'No, really, it's nothing.'

She gave a little shrug of disappointment and turned her pretty face towards the Captain.

Later Mr Pinfold tried to raise the topic of burial at sea, but this was not taken up with any enthusiasm. Mr Pinfold had devoted some thought to the matter during the late afternoon. Glover had said that the stewards came from Travancore, in which case there was a good chance of their being Christians of one or other of the ancient rites that prevailed in that complex culture. They would insist on some religious observance for one of their number. If he wished to avert suspicion, the Captain could not bundle the body overboard secretly. Once in a troopship Mr Pinfold had assisted at the committal to the sea of one of his troop who shot himself.

The business he remembered took some time. Last Post had
been sounded. Mr Pinfold rather thought the ship had hove-
to. In the *Caliban* the sports-deck seemed the most likely place
for the ceremony. Mr Pinfold would keep watch. If the night
passed without incident, Captain Steerforth would stand
acquitted.

That evening, as on the evening before, Captain Steerforth
played bridge. He smiled continuously rubber after rubber.
Early hours were kept in the *Caliban*. The bar shut at half past
ten, lights began to be turned off and ash trays emptied;
the passengers went to their cabins. Mr Pinfold saw the last of
them go below, then went aft to a seat overlooking the sports-
deck. It was very cold. He went down to his cabin for an
overcoat. It was warm there and welcoming. It occurred to
him he could keep his vigil perfectly well below deck. When
the engines stopped, he would know that the game was on.
The last faint cobwebs of his sleeping-draught had now been
swept up. He was wide awake. Without undressing he lay on
his bunk with a novel.

Time passed. No sound came through the intercommunication; the engines beat regularly, the plates and
panelling creaked; the low hum of the ventilator filled the
cabin.

There were no funeral obsequies, no panegyric; no dirge
on board the *Caliban* that night. Instead there was enacted on
the deck immediately outside Mr Pinfold's window a dra-
matic cycle lasting five hours – six? Mr Pinfold did not notice
the time at which the disturbance began – of which he was
the solitary audience. Had it appeared behind footlights on a
real stage, Mr Pinfold would have condemned it as grossly
overplayed.

There were two chief actors, juvenile leads, one of whom
was called Fosker; the other, the leader, was nameless. They

were drunk when they first arrived and presumably carried a
bottle from which they often swigged for the long hours of
darkness were of no avail in sobering them. They raged more
and more furiously until their final lapse into incoherence.
By their voices they seemed to be gentlemen of a sort. Fosker,
Mr Pinfold was pretty sure, had been in the jazz band; he
thought he had noticed him in the lounge after dinner,
amusing the girls, tall, very young, shabby, shady, vivacious,
bohemian, with long hair, a moustache, and the beginning of
side-whiskers. There was something in him of the dissolute
law students and government clerks of mid-Victorian fiction.
Something too of the young men who had now and then
crossed his path during the war – the sort of subaltern who was
disliked in his regiment and got himself posted to S.O.E.
When Mr Pinfold came to consider the matter at leisure he
could not explain to himself how he had formed so full an
impression during a brief, incurious glance, or why Fosker, if
he were what he seemed, should be travelling to the East in
such incongruous company. The image of him, however,
remained sharp cut as a cameo. The second, dominant young
man was a voice only; rather a pleasant well-bred voice for
all its vile utterances.

'He's gone to bed,' said Fosker.

'We'll soon get him out,' said the pleasant well-bred
voice.

'Music.'

'Music.'

> *'I'm Gilbert, the filbert,*
> *The knut with the K,*
> *The pride of Piccadilly,*
> *The blasé roué.*
> *Oh Hades, the ladies*

> *Who leave their wooden huts*
> *For Gilbert, the filbert,*
> *The Colonel of the Knuts.*'

'Come on, Gilbert. Time to leave your wooden hut.'

Damned impudence, thought Mr Pinfold. Oafs, bores.

'D'you think he's enjoying this?'

'He's got a most peculiar sense of humour. He's a most peculiar man. Queer, aren't you, Gilbert? Come out of your wooden hut, you old queer.'

Mr Pinfold drew the wooden shutter across his window but the noise outside was undiminished.

'He thinks that'll keep us out. It won't, Gilbert. We aren't going to climb through the window, you know. We shall come in at the door and then, by God, you're going to cop it. Now he's locked the door.' Mr Pinfold had done no such thing. 'Not very brave, is he? Locking himself in. Gilbert doesn't want to be whipped.'

'But he's going to be whipped.'

'Oh yes, he's going to be whipped all right.'

Mr Pinfold decided on action. He put on his dressing-gown, took his blackthorn, and left his cabin. The door which led out to the deck was some way down the corridor. The voices of the two hooligans followed him as he went to it. He thought he knew the Fosker type, the aggressive under-dog, vainglorious in drink, very easily put in his place. He pushed open the heavy door and stepped resolutely into the wind. The deck was quite empty. For the length of the ship the damp planks shone in the lamp-light. From above came shrieks of laughter.

'No, no, Gilbert, you can't catch us that way. Go back to your little hut, Gilbert. We'll come for you when we want you. Better lock the door.'

Mr Pinfold returned to his cabin. He did not lock the door. He sat, stick in hand, listening.

The two young men conferred.

'We'd better wait till he goes to sleep.'

'Then we'll pounce.'

'He doesn't seem very sleepy.'

'Let's get the girls to sing him to sleep. Come on, Margaret, give Gilbert a song.'

'Aren't you being rather beastly?' The girl's voice was clear and sober.

'No, of course not. It's all a joke. Gilbert's a sport. Gilbert's enjoying it as much as we are. He often did this sort of thing when he was our age – singing ridiculous songs outside men's rooms at Oxford. He made a row outside the Dean's rooms. That's why he got sent down. He accused the Dean of the most disgusting practices. It was all a great joke.'

'Well, if you're sure he doesn't mind . . .'

Two girls began singing very prettily.

> 'When first I saw Mable,
> In her fair Russian sable
> I knew she was able
> To satisfy me.
> Her manners were careless . . .'

The later lines of the song – one well known to Mr Pinfold – are verbally bawdy, but as they rose now on the passionless, true voices of the girls, they were purged and sweetened; they floated over the sea in perfect innocence. The girls sang this and other airs. They sang for a long time. They sang intermittently throughout the night's disturbances, but they were powerless to soothe Mr Pinfold. He sat wide awake with his stick to deal with intruders.

Presently the father of the nameless young man came to join them. He was, it appeared, one of the generals.

'Go to bed, you two,' he said. 'You're making an infernal nuisance of yourselves.'

'We're only mocking Pinfold. He's a beastly man.'

'That's no reason to wake up the whole ship.'

'He's a Jew.'

'Is he? Are you sure? I never heard that.'

'Of course he is. He came to Lychpole in 1937 with the German refugees. He was called Peinfeld then.'

'We're out for Peinfeld's blood,' said the pleasant voice. 'We want to beat Hell out of him.'

'You don't really mind, do you, sir,' said Fosker, 'if we beat Hell out of him.'

'What's wrong with the fellow particularly?'

'He's got a dozen pair of shoes in his little hut, all beautifully polished on wooden trees.'

'He sits at the Captain's table.'

'He's taken the only bathroom near our cabin. I tried to use it tonight and the steward said it was private, for Mr Pinfold.'

'Mr Peinfeld.'

'I hate him. I hate him. I hate him. I hate him. I hate him,' said Fosker. 'I've got my own score to settle with him for what he did to Hill.'

'That farmer who shot himself?'

'Hill was a decent, old-fashioned yeoman. The salt of the country. Then this filthy Jew came and bought up the property. The Hills had farmed it for generations. They were thrown out. That's why Hill hanged himself.'

'Well,' said the general. 'You won't do any good by shouting outside his window.'

'We're going to do more than that. We're going to give him the hiding of his life.'

'Yes, you could do that, of course.'

'You leave him to us.'

'I'm certainly not going to stay up here and be a witness. He's just the sort of fellow to take legal action.'

'He'd be far too ashamed. Can't you see the headlines, "Novelist whipped in liner"?'

'I don't suppose he'd care a damn. Fellows like that live on publicity.' Then the general changed his tone. 'All the same,' he added wistfully, 'I wish I was young enough to help, good luck to you. Give it to him good and strong. Only remember: if there's trouble, *I* know nothing about it.'

The girls sang. The youths drank. Presently the mother came to plead. She spoke in yearning tones that reminded Mr Pinfold of his deceased Anglican aunts.

'I can't sleep,' she said. 'You know I can never sleep when you're in this state. My son, I beg you to go to bed. Mr Fosker, how can you lead him into this escapade? Margaret, darling, what are you doing here at this time of night? *Please* go to your cabin, child.'

'It's only a joke, mama.'

'I very much doubt whether Mr Pinfold thinks it a joke.'

'I hate him,' said her son.

'Hate?' said the mother. 'Hate? Why do all you young people *hate* so much. What has come over the world? You were not brought up to *hate*. Why do you hate Mr Pinfold?'

'I have to share a cabin with Fosker. That swine has a cabin to himself.'

'I expect he paid for it.'

'Yes, with the money he cheated Hill out of.'

'He behaved badly to Hill certainly. But he isn't used to country ways. I've not met him, though we have lived so near all these years. I think perhaps he rather looks down on all of us. We aren't so clever as he, nor as rich. But that's no reason to *hate* him.'

At this the son broke into a diatribe in the course of which he and Fosker were left alone. There had been an element of jollity in the pair at the beginning of their demonstration. Now they were possessed by hatred, repeating and elaborating a ferocious, rambling denunciation full of obscenities. The eviction of Hill and responsibility for his suicide were the chief recurring charges but interspersed with them were other accusations. Mr Pinfold, they said, had let his mother die in destitution. He was ashamed of her because she was an illiterate immigrant, had refused to help her or go near her, had let her die alone, uncared for, had not attended her pauper's funeral. Mr Pinfold had shirked in the war. He had used it as an opportunity to change his name and pass himself off as an Englishman, to make friends with people who did not know his origin, to get into Bellamy's Club. Mr Pinfold had in some way been implicated in the theft of a moonstone. He had paid a large sum of money to sit at the Captain's table. Mr Pinfold typified the decline of England, of rural England in particular. He was a reincarnation (Mr Pinfold, not they, drew the analogy) of the 'new men' of the Tudor period who had despoiled the Church and the peasantry. His religious profession was humbug, assumed in order to ingratiate himself with the aristocracy. Mr Pinfold was a sodomite. Mr Pinfold must be chastened and chastised.

The night wore on, the charges became wilder and wider, the threats more bloody. The two young men were like prancing savages working themselves into a frenzy of blood-lust. Mr Pinfold awaited their attack and prepared for it. He made an operational plan. They would come through the door singly. The cabin was not spacious but there was room to swing a stick. He turned out the light and stood by the door.

The young men coming suddenly into the dark from the lighted corridor would not know where to lay hands on him. He would fell the first with his blackthorn, then change this weapon for the malacca cane. The second young man no doubt would stumble over his fallen friend. Mr Pinfold would then turn on the light and carefully thrash him. They were far too drunk to be really dangerous. Mr Pinfold was quite confident of the outcome. He awaited them calmly.

The incantations were rising to a climax.

'Now's the time. Ready, Fosker?'

'Ready.'

'In we go then.'

'You first, Fosker.'

Mr Pinfold stood ready. He was glad that Fosker should be the man to be painlessly stunned; the instigator, the man to receive full punishment. There was justice in that order.

Then came anticlimax. 'I can't get in,' said Fosker. 'The bastard has locked the door.'

Mr Pinfold had not locked the door. Moreover Fosker had not tried it. There had been no movement of the handle. Fosker was afraid.

'Go on. What are you waiting for?'

'I tell you he's locked us out.'

'That's torn it.'

Crestfallen, the two returned to the deck.

'We've got to get him. We must get him tonight,' said the one who was not Fosker, but the fire had gone out of him and he added: 'I feel awfully sick suddenly.'

'Better put it off for tonight.'

'I feel frightful. Oh!'

There followed the ghastly sounds of vomiting and then a whimper; the same abject sound that seemed to re-echo through the *Caliban*, the sob of the injured seaman, of the murdered steward.

His mother was there now to comfort him.

'I haven't been to bed, dear. I couldn't leave you like that. I've been waiting and praying for you. You're ready to come now, aren't you?'

'Yes, mother. I'm ready.'

'I love you so. All loving is suffering.'

Silence fell. Mr Pinfold put his weapons away and drew back the shutter. It was dawn. He lay on his bed wide awake, his rage quite abated, calmly considering the events of the night.

There had been no funeral. So much seemed certain. Indeed the whole incident of Captain Steerforth and Goneril and the murdered steward had become insubstantial under the impact of the new assault. Mr Pinfold's orderly, questing mind began to sift the huge volume of charges which had been made against him. Some – that he was Jewish and homosexual, that he had stolen a moonstone and left his mother to die a pauper – were totally preposterous. Others were inconsistent. If, for example, he were a newly arrived immigrant, he could not have been a rowdy undergraduate at Oxford; if he were so anxious to establish himself as a countryman, he would not have slighted his neighbours. The young men in their drunken rage had clearly roared out any abuse that came to mind, but there emerged from the chaotic uproar the basic facts that he was generally disliked on board the *Caliban*, that two at least of his fellow-passengers were possessed by fanatical hate, and that they had some sort of indirect personal acquaintance with him. How else could they have heard, even in its wildly garbled form, of his wife's transactions with Hill (who was well and prosperous when Mr Pinfold last heard of him)? They came from his part of the country. It was not unlikely that Hill, while boasting of his astuteness among his cronies, had told a story of oppression elsewhere. If that was the sort of thing that was being said in the district, Mr Pinfold should correct it. Mr Pinfold had to consider also his comfort during the coming voyage. He required peace of mind in which to work. These dreadful young men were likely, whenever they got drunk, to come caterwauling outside his cabin. On a later occasion, moreover, they might attempt physical assault, might even succeed in it. The result could only be humiliating; it might be painful. The world teemed with journalists. He imagined his wife reading in her morning paper a cable from Aden or Port Soudan describing the *fracas*. Something must be done. He could lay the matter before the Captain, the natural guardian of law in his ship, but with this thought there emerged again from oblivion the matter of the Captain's own culpability. Mr Pinfold was going to have the Captain arrested for murder at the earliest opportunity. Nothing would suit that black heart better than to have the only witness against him involved in a brawl – or silenced in one. A new suspicion took shape. Mr Pinfold had been indiscreet at dinner in revealing his private knowledge. Was it not probable that Captain Steerforth had instigated the whole attack? Where had the young men been drinking after the bar was shut, if not in the Captain's cabin?

Mr Pinfold began to shave. This prosaic operation recalled him to strict reason. The Captain's guilt was not proven. First things first. He must deal with the young men. He studied the passenger-list. There was no Fosker on it. Mr Pinfold himself, when crossing the Atlantic, avoided interviewers by remaining incognito. It seemed unlikely that Fosker would have the same motive. Perhaps the police were after him. The other man was ostensibly respectable; four of a name should be easy to find. But there seemed to be no family of father, mother, son, and daughter in that list. Mr Pinfold lathered his face for the second shave. He was puzzled. It was unlikely that so large a party would join the ship at the last moment, after the list had been printed. They did not sound the kind of people given to impetuous dashes abroad – and anyway, such people travelled by air nowadays. And there was that other general travelling with them. Mr Pinfold gazed at his puzzled, soapy face. Then he saw light. Stepfather, that was it. He and the mother would bear one name, the children another. Mr Pinfold would keep his eyes and ears open. It should not be difficult to identify them.

Mr Pinfold dressed carefully. He chose a Brigade tie to wear that morning and a cap that matched his tweed suit. He went on deck, where seamen were at work swabbing. They had already cleaned up all traces of the night's disgusting climax. He ascended to the main, promenade deck. It was a morning such as at any other time would have elated him. Even now, with so much to harass him, he was conscious of exhilaration. He stood alone breathing deeply, making light of his annoyances.

Margaret, somewhere quite near, said: 'Look, he's left his cabin. Doesn't he look smart today? Now's our chance to give him our presents. It's much better than giving them to his steward as we meant to. Now we can arrange them ourselves.'

'D'you think he'll like them?' said the other girl.

'He ought to. We've taken enough trouble. They're the best we could possibly get.'

'But Meg, he's so *grand*.'

'It's because he's grand he'll like them. Grand people are always pleased with *little* things. He *must* have his presents this morning. After the silly way the boys behaved last night it

will show him *we* weren't in it. At least not in it in the way
they were. He'll see that as far as we're concerned it was all fun
and love.'

'Suppose he comes in and finds us?'

'You keep *cave*. If he starts going down sing.'

'"When first I saw Mabel"?'

'Of course. *Our* song.'

Mr Pinfold was tempted to trap Margaret. He relished the
simple male pleasure, rather rare to him in recent years, of
being found attractive, and was curious to see this honey-
tongued girl. But she inevitably would lead him to the brother
and to Fosker, and he was constrained by honour. These
presents, whatever they were, constituted a flag of truce. He
could not snatch advantage from the girls' generosity.

Presently Margaret rejoined her friend.

'He hasn't moved.'

'No, he's just stood there all the time. What do you suppose
he's thinking about?'

'Those beastly boys, I expect.'

'Do you think he's very upset?'

'He's so brave.'

'Often brave people are the most sensitive.'

'Well it will be all right when he gets back to his cabin and
finds our presents.'

Mr Pinfold walked the decks for an hour. No passengers
were about.

As the gong sounded for breakfast, Mr Pinfold went below.
He stopped first at his cabin to see what Margaret had left for
him. All he found was the cup of tea, cold now, which the
steward had put there. The bed was made. The place was
squared up and shipshape. There were no presents.

As he left, he met the cabin-steward.

'I say, did a young lady leave anything for me in my cabin?'

'Yes, sir, breakfast now, sir.'

'No. Listen. I think something was left for me here about an hour ago.'

'Yes, sir, gong for breakfast just now.'

'Oh,' said Margaret, 'he hasn't found it.'

'He must *look*.'

'*Look* for it, Gilbert, *look*.'

He searched the little wardrobe. He peered under the bunk. He opened the cupboard over the wash-hand-basin. There was nothing there.

'There's nothing there,' said Margaret. 'He can't find it. He can't find anything,' she said on a soft note of despair. 'The sweet brave idiot, he can't find anything.'

So he went down alone to breakfast.

He was the first of the passengers to appear. Mr Pinfold was hungry. He ordered coffee and fish and eggs and fruit. He was about to eat when, Ping; the little, rose-shaded electric lamp which stood on the table before him came into action as a transmitter. The delinquent youths were awake and up on the air again, their vitality unimpaired by the excesses of the night.

'Halloo-loo-loo-loo-loo. Hark-ark-ark-ark-ark,' they holloaed. 'Loo in there. Fetch him out. Yoicks.'

'I fear Fosker is not entirely conversant with sporting parlance,' said the general.

'Hark-ark-ark-ark. Come out, Peinfeld. We know where you are. We've got you.' A whip-crack. 'Ow,' from Fosker, 'look out what you're doing with that hunting crop.'

'Run, Peinfeld, run. We can see you. We're coming for you.'

The steward at that moment was at Mr Pinfold's side serving

him with haddock. He seemed unconscious of the cries emanating from the lamp; to him presumably they were all one with the unreasonable variety of knives and forks and the superfluity of inedible foods; all part of the complexity of this remote and rather disgusting Western way of life.

Mr Pinfold ate stolidly. The young men resumed the diatribe repeating again in clear, morning voices the garbled accusations of the night before. Interspersed with them was the challenge: 'Come and meet us, Gilbert. You're afraid, Peinfeld. We want to talk to you, Peinfeld. You're hiding, aren't you? You're afraid to come and talk.'

Margaret spoke: 'Oh, Gilbert, what are they doing to you? Where are you? You mustn't let them find you. Come to me. I'll hide you. You never found your presents and now they are after you again. Let *me* look after you, Gilbert. It's me, Mimi. Don't you trust me?'

Mr Pinfold turned to his scrambled eggs. He had forgotten, when he ordered them, that they would not be fresh. Now he beckoned to the steward to remove them.

'Off your feed, Gilbert? You're in a funk, aren't you? Can't eat when you're in a funk, can you? Poor Gilbert, too scared to eat.' They began to give instructions for a place of meeting. '. . . D Deck, turn right. Got that? You'll see some lockers. The next bulk-head. We're waiting for you. Better come now and get it over. You've got to meet us some time, you know. We've got you, Gilbert. We've got you. There's no escape. Better get it over . . .'

Mr Pinfold's patience was exhausted. He must put a stop to this nonsense. Recalling some vague memories of signal procedure in the army, he drew the lamp towards him and spoke into it curtly: 'Pinfold to Hooligans. Rendezvous Main Lounge 0930 hours. Out.'

The lamp was not designed to be moved. His pull disconnected it in some way. The bulb went out and the voices abruptly ceased. At the same moment Glover came in to breakfast. 'Hullo, something gone wrong with the light?'

'I tried to move it. I hope you slept better last night?'

'Like a log. No more disturbances, I hope?'

Mr Pinfold considered whether or not to confide in Glover and decided immediately, no.

'No,' he said, and ordered some cold ham.

The dining-saloon filled. Mr Pinfold exchanged greetings. He went on deck, keeping alert, hoping to spot his persecutors, thinking it possible that Margaret would make herself known to him. But he saw no hooligans; half a dozen healthy girls passed him, some in trousers and duffle coats, some in tweed skirts and sweaters; one might be Margaret but none gave him a sign. At half past nine he took an armchair in a corner of the lounge and waited. He had his blackthorn with him; it was just conceivable that the youths were so frenzied that they might attempt violence even here, in the daylight.

He began to rehearse the coming interview. He was the judge. He had summoned these men to appear before him. Something like a regimental orderly room, he thought, would be the proper atmosphere. He was the commanding officer hearing a charge of brawling. His powers of punishment were meagre. He would admonish them severely, and threaten them with civil penalties.

He would remind them that they were subject to British law in the *Caliban* just as much as on land; that defamation of character and physical assault were grave crimes which would prejudice their whole future careers. He would 'throw the whole book' at them. He would explain icily that he was entirely indifferent to their good or bad opinion; that he regarded their friendship and their enmity as equally impertinent. But he would also hear what they had to say for themselves. A good officer knows the enormous ills that can arise from men brooding on imaginary grudges. These defaulters were clearly suffering from a number of delusions about himself. It was better that they should get it off their chests, hear the truth, and then shut up for the rest of the voyage. Moreover if, as seemed certain, these delusions derived from rumours which were in circulation among Mr Pinfold's neighbours, he must plainly investigate and scotch them.

He had the lounge to himself. The rest of the passengers were ranged along the deck in their chairs and rugs. The unvarying hum of marine mechanical-life was the only sound. The clock over the little bandstand read a quarter to ten. Mr Pinfold decided to give them till ten; then he would go to the wireless office and inform his wife of his recovery. It was beneath his dignity to attend on these dreadful young men.

Some similar point of pride seemed to influence them. Above the hum he presently heard them discussing him. The voices came from the panelling near his head. First in his cabin, then in the dining-saloon, now here, the surviving strands of wartime intercommunication were fitfully active. The whole wiring of the ship was in need of a thorough overhaul, Mr Pinfold thought; for all he knew there might be a danger of fire.

'We'll talk to Peinfeld when it suits us and not a moment before.'

'Who'll do the talking?'

'I will, of course.'

'Do you know what you're going to say?'

'Of course.'

'Not really much point in my coming at all, is there?'

'I may need you as a witness.'

'All right, come on then. Let's see him now.'

'When it suits *me*, Fosker, not before.'

'What are we waiting for?'

'To let him get into a thorough funk. Remember at school one was always kept waiting for a beating? Just to make it taste sweeter? Well, Peinfeld can wait for *his* beating.'

'He's scared stiff.'

'He's practically blubbing now.'

At ten o'clock Mr Pinfold took out his watch, verified the time shown on the clock, and rose from the corner. 'He's going away.' 'He's running away.' 'Funk' came faintly from the fumed oak panelling. Mr Pinfold climbed to the wireless office on the boat-deck, composed a message and handed it in: *Pinfold. Lychpole. Entirely cured. All love. Gilbert.*

'Is that address enough?' asked the clerk.

'Yes. There's only one telegraph office called Lychpole in the country.'

He walked the decks, thought his blackthorn superfluous and returned to his cabin where the B.B.C. was loudly in possession. '. . . in the studio Jimmy Lance, who is well known to all listeners, and Miss June Cumberleigh, who is new to listeners. Jimmy is going to let us see what is probably a unique collection. He has kept every letter he ever received. That's so, isn't it, Jimmy?'

'Well, not letters from the Income Tax Collector.'

'Ha. Ha.'

'Ha. Ha.'

A great burst of unrestrained laughter from the unseen audience.

'No, none of us like to be reminded of that kind of letter, Jimmy, do we? Ha ha. But I think in your time you have had letters from a great many celebrities?'

'And from some pretty dim people, too.'

'Ha. Ha.'

'Ha. Ha. Ha.'

'Well, June is going to take letters at random out of your file and read them. Ready, June? Right. The first letter is from – '

Mr Pinfold knew June Cumberleigh and liked her. She was a wholly respectable, clever, funny-faced girl who had got drawn into Bohemia through her friendship with James Lance. It was not her natural voice that she now used. Through some mechanical distortion she spoke in almost identical tones to Goneril's.

'Gilbert Pinfold,' she said.

'And do you count him among the celebrities or the dim people, Jimmy?'

'A celebrity.'

'Do you?' said June. 'I think he's a dreadfully dim little man.'

'Well, what's the dim little man got to say?'

'It is so badly written I can't read it.'

Enormous amusement in the audience.

'Try another.'

'Who is it this time?'

'Why. This is *too* much. Gilbert Pinfold again.'

'Ha, ha, ha, ha, ha.'

Mr Pinfold left his cabin, slamming the door on this deplorable entertainment. James, he knew, did a lot of broadcasting. He was a poet and artist by nature who had let himself become popularized; but this exhibition was a bit thick, even for him. And what was June doing? She must have lost all sense of decency.

Mr Pinfold walked the decks. He was still troubled by the unsolved problem of the hooligans. Something would have to be done about them. But he felt reassured about Captain Steerforth. Now that it was apparent that many of the sounds in his cabin emanated from Broadcasting House, he became certain that what he had overheard was part of a play. The similarity of June's voice and Goneril's seemed to confirm it. He had been an ass to suppose Captain Steerforth a murderer; it was part of the confusion of mind caused by Dr Drake's pills. And if Captain Steerforth were innocent, then he was a potential, a natural ally against his enemies.

Thus comforted, Mr Pinfold returned to his listening post in the corner of the lounge. Father and son were in conference.

'Fosker's wet.'

'Yes. I've never thought anything of him.'

'I'm leaving him out of this business from now on.'

'Very wise. But you've got to go through with it yourself, you know. You didn't come very creditably out of last night's affair. I've no great objection to your knocking the fellow about a bit if he deserves it. Anyway you've threatened him and you've got to do something about it. You can't just drop the matter at this stage. But you want to go about it in the right way. You're up against something rather more dangerous than you realize.'

'Dangerous? That cowardly, common little communist pansy –'

'Yes, yes. I know how you feel. But I've seen a bit more of the world than you have, my boy. I think I'd better put you up to a few wrinkles. In the first place Pinfold is utterly unscrupulous. He has no gentlemanly instincts. He's quite capable of taking you to the courts. Have you any proof of your charges?'

'Everyone knows they're true.'

'That may be but it won't mean a thing in a court of law unless you can prove it. You need evidence so strong that Pinfold daren't sue you. And, so far, you haven't got it. Another thing, Pinfold is extremely rich. I daresay for example he owns a controlling share in this shipping line. The long-nosed, curly-headed gentlemen don't pay taxes like us poor Christians, you know. Pinfold has money salted away in half a dozen countries. He has friends everywhere.'

'Friends?'

'Well, no, not friends as *we* understand them. But he has influence – with politicians, with the police. You've lived in a small world, my boy. You have no conception of the ramifications of power of a man like Pinfold in the modern age. He's attractive to women – homosexuals always are. Margaret is distinctly taken with him. Even your mother doesn't really dislike him. We've got to work cautiously and build up a party against him. I'll send off a few radiograms. There are one or two people I know who, I think, may be able to give us some *facts* about Pinfold. It's facts we need. We've got to make out an absolutely water-tight case. Till then, lie low.'

'You don't think I ought to beat him up?'

'Well, I wouldn't go so far as to say that. If you find him alone, you might have a smack at him. I know what I should have done myself at your age. But I'm old now and wise and my advice is lie low, work under cover. Then in a day or two we may have something to surprise our celebrated fellow passenger ...'

When noon was sounded Mr Pinfold went aft and ordered himself a cocktail. There was the usual jollity over the sweep-stake. He looked at the flag on the chart. The *Caliban* had rounded Cape St Vincent and was well on the way to Gibraltar. She should pass the straits that night into the Mediterranean. When he went down to luncheon he was in a hopeful mood. The hooligans had fallen out and their rage had been tempered. The Mediterranean had always welcomed Mr

Pinfold in the past. His annoyance would be over, he believed, once he was in those hallowed waters.

In the dining-saloon he noticed that the dark man who had sat alone was now at a table with Mrs Cockson and Mrs Benson. In a curious way that too seemed a good omen.

5

THE INTERNATIONAL INCIDENT

IT was the conversation of the two generals, overheard as he lay in his cabin after luncheon, which first made Mr Pinfold aware of the international crisis which had been developing while he lay ill. There had been no hint of it in the newspapers he had listlessly scanned before embarkation; or, if there had been, he had not, in his confused state, appreciated its importance. Now, it appeared, there was a first-class row about the possession of Gibraltar. Some days ago the Spaniards had laid formal, peremptory claim to the fortress and were now exercising the very dubious right of stopping and searching ships passing through the straits in what they defined as their territorial waters. During luncheon the *Caliban* had hove-to and Spanish officials had come on board. They were demanding that the ship put into Algeciras for an examination of cargo and passengers.

The two generals were incensed against General Franco and made free use of 'tin-pot dictator', 'twopenny-halfpenny Hitler', 'dago', 'priest-ridden puppet', and similar opprobrious epithets. They also spoke contemptuously of the British government who were prepared to 'truckle' to him.

'It's nothing short of a blockade. If I were in command I'd call their bluff, go full steam ahead and tell them to shoot and be damned.'

'That would be an act of war, of course.'

'Serve 'em right. We haven't sunk so low that we can't lick the Spaniards, I hope.'

'It's all this UNO.'

'And the Americans.'

'Anyway, this is one thing that can't be blamed on Russia.'

'It means the end of NATO.'

'Good riddance.'

'The Captain has to take his orders from home, I suppose.'

'That's the trouble. He can't get any orders.'

Captain Steerforth was now fully restored to Mr Pinfold's confidence. He saw him as a simple sailor obliged to make a momentous decision, not only for the safety of his own vessel but for the peace of the world. Throughout that long afternoon Mr Pinfold followed the frantic attempts of the signalmen to get into touch with the shipping company, the Foreign Office, the Governor of Gibraltar, the Mediterranean fleet. All were without avail. Captain Steerforth stood quite alone as the representative of international justice and British prestige. Mr Pinfold thought of Jenkins's ear and the Private of the Buffs. Captain Steerforth was a good man forced into an importance quite beyond his capabilities. Mr Pinfold wished he could stand beside him on the bridge, exhort him to defiance, run the ship under the Spanish guns into the wide, free inland sea where all the antique heroes of history and legend had sailed to glory.

As factions resolve in common danger, Mr Pinfold forgot the enmity of the young hooligans. All on board the *Caliban* were comrades-in-arms against foreign aggression.

The Spanish officials were polite enough. Mr Pinfold could hear them talking in the Captain's cabin. In excellent English they explained how deeply repugnant they, personally, found the orders they had to carry out. It was a question of politics, they said. No doubt the matter would be adjusted satisfactorily at a congress. Meanwhile they could only obey. They spoke of some enormous indemnity which, if it were forthcoming from London, would immediately ensure the *Cali-ban*'s free passage. A time was mentioned, midnight, after which, if no satisfactory arrangements were made, the *Caliban* would be taken under escort to Algeciras.

'Piracy,' said Captain Steerforth, 'blackmail.'

'We cannot allow such language about the Head of the State.'

'Then you can bloody well get off my bridge,' said the Captain. They withdrew but nothing was settled by the tiff. They remained on board and the ship lay motionless.

Towards evening Mr Pinfold went on deck. There was no sign of land, nor of the Spanish ship which had brought the officials and, presumably, was lying off somewhere below the horizon. Mr Pinfold leaned over the rail and looked down at the flowing sea. The sun was dead astern of them sinking low over the water. Had he not known better, he would have supposed they were still steaming forward, so swiftly and steadily ran the current. He recalled that he had once been taught that through the Suez Canal the Indian Ocean emptied itself into the Atlantic. He thought of the multitudinous waters that supplied the Mediterranean, the ice-flows of the Black Sea that raced past Constantinople and Troy; the great rivers of history, the Nile, the Euphrates, the Danube, the Rhône. They it was that broke across the bows and left a foaming wake.

The passengers seemed quite unaware of the doom which threatened the ship. Fresh from their siestas they sat about that afternoon just as they had sat before, reading and talking and knitting. There was the same little group on the sports-deck. Mr Pinfold met Glover.

'Did you see the Spaniards come on board?' he asked.

'Spaniards? Come on board? How could they? When?'

'They're causing a lot of trouble.'

'I'm awfully sorry,' said Glover. 'I simply don't know what you're talking about.'

'You will,' said Mr Pinfold. 'Soon enough I fear.'

Glover looked at him with the keen, perplexed air which he often assumed now when Mr Pinfold spoke to him.

'There aren't any Spaniards on board that I know of.'

It was not Mr Pinfold's duty to spread alarm and despondency or explain his unique sources of information. The Captain plainly wanted the secret kept as long as possible.

'I dare say I'm mistaken,' said Mr Pinfold loyally.

'There are Burmese and the Norwegian couple at our table. They're the only foreigners I've seen.'

'Yes. A misunderstanding no doubt.'

Glover went to the space in the bows where he swung his club. He swung it methodically, with concentration, without a thought of Spaniards.

Mr Pinfold withdrew to his listening post in the corner of the lounge but nothing was to be heard there except the tapping of morse as the signalmen sent out their calls for help. One of them said: 'Nothing coming in at all. I don't believe our signals are going out.'

'It's that new device,' said his mate. 'I heard something had been invented to create wireless silence. It's not been tried before, as far as I know. It was develped too late to use in the war. Both sides were at work on it but it was still in the experimental stage in 1945.'

'More effective than jamming.'

'Different principle altogether. They can only do it at short range so far. In a year or two it'll develop so that they can isolate whole countries.'

'Where will our jobs be then?'

'Oh, someone'll find a counter-system. They always do.'

'Anyway all we can do now is keep on trying.'

The tapping recommenced. Mr Pinfold went to the bar and ordered himself a glass of gin and bitters. The English steward came in from the deck, tray in hand, and went to the serving hatch.

'Those Spanish bastards are asking for whisky,' he said.

'I'll not serve them,' said the man who handled the bottles.

'Captain's order,' said the steward.

'What's come over the old man? It isn't like him to take a thing like this lying down.'

'He's got a plan. Trust him. Now give me those four whiskies and I hope it poisons them.'

Mr Pinfold finished his drink and returned to his listening post. He was curious to know more of the Captain's plan. He had no sooner settled in his chair and attuned his ear to the panelling than he heard the Captain; he was in his cabin addressing the officers.

'. . . all questions of international law and convention apart,' he was saying, 'there is a particular reason why we cannot allow this ship to be searched. You all know we have an extra man on board. He's not a passenger. He's not one of the crew. He doesn't appear on any list. He's got no ticket or papers. I don't even know his name myself. I daresay you've noticed him sitting alone in the dining-saloon. All I've been told is that he's very important indeed to H.M.G. He's on a special mission. That's why he's travelling with us instead of on one of the routes that are watched. It's him, of course, that the Spaniards are after. All this talk about territorial waters and right of search is pure bluff. We've got to see that that man gets through.'

'How are you going to manage that, skipper?'

'I don't know yet. But I've got an idea. I think I shall have to take the passengers into my confidence – not all of them, of course, and not fully into my confidence. But I'm going

to collect half a dozen of the more responsible men and put
them into the picture – into a bit of the picture anyway. I'll
ask them up here, casually, after dinner. With their help the
plan *may* work.'

The generals received their invitation early and were not
deceived by its casual form. They were discussing it while Mr
Pinfold dressed for dinner.

'It looks as though he's decided to put up a fight.'

'We'll all stand by him.'

'Can we trust those Burmese?'

'That's a question to raise at the meeting tonight.'

'Wouldn't trust 'em myself. Yellow-bellies.'

'The Norwegians?'

'They seem sound enough but this is a British affair.'

'Always happier on our own, eh?'

It did not occur to Mr Pinfold that he might be omitted
from the Captain's *cadre*. But no invitation reached him
although in various other parts of the ship he heard confidential messages ... 'the Captain's compliments and he would be
grateful if you could find it convenient to come to his cabin
for a few minutes after dinner ...'

At table Captain Steerforth carried his anxieties with splendid composure. Mrs Scarfield actually asked him: 'When do
we go through the straits?' and he replied without any
perceptible nuance: 'Early tomorrow morning.'

'It ought to get warmer then?'

'Not at this time of year,' he answered nonchalantly. 'You
must wait for the Red Sea before you go into whites.'

During their brief acquaintance Mr Pinfold had regarded
this man with sharply varying emotions. Unquestionable
admiration filled him when, at the end of dinner, Mrs Scarfield asked: 'Are you joining us for a rubber?' and he replied:
'Not this evening, I'm afraid. I've one or two things to see

to,' but though Mr Pinfold hung back so that he left the dining-saloon at the Captain's side, giving him the chance to invite him to the conference, they parted at the head of the stair without the word being said. Rather nonplussed Mr Pinfold hesitated, then decided to go to his cabin. It was essential that he should be easily found when he was wanted.

Soon it was apparent that he was not wanted at all. Captain Steerforth had his party promptly assembled and he began by giving them a résumé of the situation as Mr Pinfold already understood it. He said nothing of the secret agent. He merely explained that he had been unable to obtain authorization from his company to pay the preposterous sum demanded. The alternative offered by the Spaniards was that he should put into Algeciras until the matter had been settled between Madrid and London. That, he said, would be a betrayal of every standard of British seamanship. The *Caliban* would not strike her flag. There was a burst of restrained, husky, emotional, male applause. He explained his plan: at midnight the Spanish ship would come alongside. The officials now on board would trans-ship to her to report the results of their demand. They intended to take with them under arrest himself and a party of hostages and to put an officer of their own on his bridge to sail her into the Spanish port. It was in the dark, on the gangway, that the resistance would disclose itself. The English would overpower the Spaniards, throw them back into their ship – 'and if one or two go into the drink in the process, so much the better' – and the *Caliban* would then make full steam ahead. 'I don't think when it comes to the point, they'll open fire. Anyway their gunnery is pretty moderate and I consider it's a risk we have to take. You are all agreed?'

'Agreed. Agreed. Agreed.'

'I knew I could trust you,' said the Captain. 'You're all

men who've seen service. I am proud to have you under my command. The yellow-bellies will be locked in their cabins.'

'How about Pinfold?' asked one of the generals. 'Shouldn't he be here?'

'There is a role assigned to Captain Pinfold. I don't think I need to go into that at the moment.'

'Has he received his orders?'

'Not yet,' said Captain Steerforth. 'We have some hours before us. I suggest, gentlemen, that you go about the ship in the normal way, turn in early, and rendezvous here at 11.45. Midnight is zero hour. Perhaps, general, you will remain behind for a few minutes. For the present, good night, gentlemen.'

The meeting broke up. Presently only the general remained with the first and second officers in the Captain's cabin.

'Well,' said Captain Steerforth, 'how did that sound?'

'Pretty thin, skipper, if you ask me,' said the first officer.

'I take it,' said the general, 'that what we have just heard was merely the cover-plan?'

'Precisely. I could hardly hope to deceive an old campaigner like you. I am sorry not to be able to take your companions into my confidence, but in the interest of security I have had to limit those in the know to an absolute minimum. The role of the committee who have just left us is to create sufficient diversion to enable us to carry out the real purpose of the operation. That, of course, is to prevent a certain person falling into the hands of the enemy.'

'Pinfold?'

'No, no, quite the contrary. Captain Pinfold, I fear, has to be written off. The Spaniards will not let us pass until they think they have their man. It has not been an easy decision, I assure you. I am responsible for the safety of all my passsengers, but at a time like this sacrifices have to be accepted. The plan briefly is this. Captain Pinfold is to impersonate the agent. He will be provided with papers identifying him. The Spaniards will take him ashore and the ship will sail on unmolested.'

There was a pause while this proposition was considered. The first officer at length spoke: 'It might work, skipper.'

'It *must* work.'

'What do you suppose will happen to him?'

'Can't say. I suppose they'll hold him under arrest while they investigate. They won't let him communicate with our embassy, of course. When they find out their mistake, if they ever do, they'll be in rather a jam. They may let him out or they may find it more convenient just to let him disappear.'

'I see.'

It was the general who voiced the thought uppermost in Mr Pinfold's mind. 'Why Pinfold?' he asked.

'It was a painful choice,' said Captain Steerforth, 'but not a difficult one. He is the obvious man, really. No one else on board would take them in for a moment. He looks like a secret agent. I think he was one during the war. He's a sick man and therefore expendable. And, of course, he's a Roman Catholic. That ought to make things a little easier for him in Spain.'

'Yes,' said the general, 'yes. I see all that. But all the same I think it's pretty sporting of him to agree. In his place I must own I'd think twice before taking it on.'

'Oh, *he* doesn't know anything about it.'

'The devil he doesn't?'

'No, that would be quite fatal to security. Besides he might *not* agree. He has a wife, you know, and a large family. You can't really blame a man who thinks of domestic responsibilities before volunteering for hazardous service. No, Captain Pinfold must be kept quite in the dark. That's the reason for the counter-plan, the diversion. There's got to be a schemozzle on the gangway so that Captain Pinfold can be pushed into the corvette. You, number one, will be responsible for hauling him out of his cabin and planting the papers on him.'

'Aye, aye, sir.'

'That boy of mine will laugh,' said the general. 'He took against Pinfold from the start. Now he hears he's deserted to the enemy . . .'

The voices ceased. For a long time Mr Pinfold sat paralysed with horror and rage. When at length he looked at his watch he found that it was nearly half past nine. Then he took off his evening clothes and put on his tweeds. Whatever outrage the night brought forth should find him suitably dressed. He pocketed his passport and his traveller's cheques. Then, blackthorn in hand, he sat down again and began patiently and painfully as he had learned in the army, to 'appreciate the situation'. He was alone, without hope of reinforcement. His sole advantage was that he knew, and they did not know he knew their plan of action. He examined the Captain's plan in the light of the quite considerable experience he had acquired in small-scale night operations and he found it derisory. The result of a scuffle in the dark on a gangway was quite unpredictable but he was confident that, forewarned, he could easily evade or repulse any attempt to put him into the corvette against his will. Even if they succeeded and the *Caliban* attempted to sail away, the corvette, of course, would open fire and, of course, would sink or disable her long before the Spaniards began examining the forged papers that were to be planted on him.

And here Mr Pinfold experienced scruples. He was not what is generally meant by the appellation a 'philanthropic' man; he totally lacked what was now called a 'social conscience'. But apart from his love of family and friends he had a certain basic kindliness to those who refrained from active annoyance. And in an old-fashioned way he was patriotic. These sentiments sometimes did service for what are generally regarded as the higher loyalties and affections. This was such an occasion. He rather liked Mrs Scarfield, Mrs Cockson, Mrs Benson, Glover, and all those simple, chatting, knitting, dozing passengers. For the unseen, enigmatic Margaret he felt tender curiosity. It would be a pity for all these to be precipitated into a watery bier by the ineptitude of Captain Steerforth. For himself he had little concern, but he knew that his disappearance, and possible disgrace, would grieve his wife and family. It was intolerable that this booby Captain should handle so many lives so clumsily. But there was also the question of the secret agent. If this man, as seemed likely, was really of vital importance to his country, he must be protected. Mr Pinfold felt responsible for his protection. He had been chosen as victim. That doom was inescapable. But he would go to the sacrifice a garlanded hero. He would not be tricked into it.

No precise tactical plan could be made. Whatever his action, it would be improvised. But the intention was plain. He would, if necessary, consent to impersonate the agent, but Captain Steerforth and his cronies must understand that he went voluntarily as a man of honour and Mrs Pinfold must be fully informed of the circumstances. That established, he would consent to his arrest.

As he pondered all this, he was barely conscious of the voices that came to him. He waited.

At a quarter to twelve there was a hail from the bridge answered from the sea in Spanish. The corvette was coming alongside and at once the ship came to life with a multitude of voices. This, Mr Pinfold decided, was his moment to act. He must deliver his terms to the Captain before the Spaniards came on board. Gripping his blackthorn he left the cabin.

Immediately his communications were cut. The lighted corridor was empty and completely silent. He strode down it to the stairway, mounted to the main deck. No one was

T-O.G.P.-D

about. There was no ship near or anywhere in sight; not a light anywhere on the dark horizon; not a sound from the bridge; only the rush and slap of the waves along the ship's side, and the keen sea wind. Mr Pinfold stood confounded, the only troubled thing in a world at peace.

He had been dauntless a minute before in the face of his enemies. Now he was struck with real fear, something totally different from the superficial alarms he had once or twice known in moments of danger, something he had quite often read about and dismissed as over-writing. He was possessed from outside himself with atavistic panic. 'O let me not be mad, not mad, sweet heaven,' he cried.

And in that moment of agony there broke not far from him in the darkness peal upon rising peal of mocking laughter – Goneril's. It was not an emollient sound. It was devoid of mirth, an obscene cacophany of pure hatred. But it fell on Mr Pinfold's ears at that moment like a nursery lullaby.

'A hoax,' he said to himself.

It was all a hoax on the part of the hooligans. He understood all. They had learned the secret of the defective wiring in his cabin. Somehow they had devised a means of controlling it, somehow they had staged this whole charade to tease him. It was spiteful and offensive, no doubt; it must not happen again. But Mr Pinfold felt nothing but gratitude in his discovery. He might be unpopular; he might be ridiculous; but he was not mad.

He returned to his cabin. He had been awake now for thirty or forty hours. He lay down at once in his clothes and fell into a deep, natural sleep. He lay motionless and unconscious for six hours.

When he next went on deck the sun was up, directly over the bows. Square on the port beam rose the unmistakable peak of the Rock. The *Caliban* was steaming into the calm Mediterranean.

6

THE HUMAN TOUCH

WHILE Mr Pinfold was shaving, he heard Margaret say: 'It was an absolutely beastly joke and I'm glad it fell flat.'

'It came off very nicely,' said her brother. 'Old Peinfeld was jibbering with funk.'

'He wasn't – and he isn't called Peinfeld. He was a hero. When I saw him standing there alone on deck I thought of Nelson.'

'He was drunk.'

'He says it's not drink, dear,' said their mother, gently uncommitted to either side. 'He *says* it's some medicine he has to take.'

'Medicine from a brandy bottle.'

'I know you're wrong,' said Margaret. 'You see it just happens *I know* what he's thinking, and you don't.'

Then Goneril's steely voice cut in: '*I* can tell you what he was doing on deck. He was screwing up his courage to jump overboard. He longs to kill himself, don't you, Gilbert. All right, I know you're listening down there. You can hear me, can't you, Gilbert? You wish you were dead, don't you, Gilbert? And a very good idea, too. Why don't you do it, Gilbert? Why not? Perfectly easy. It would save us all – you too, Gilbert – a great deal of trouble.'

'Beast,' said Margaret and broke into weeping.

'Oh, God,' said her brother, 'now you've turned on the water-works again.'

Mr Pinfold was fortified by his six hours' sleep. He went

above, leaving the nagging voices of the cabin for the silent and empty decks for an hour. The Rock had dropped below the horizon and there was no land in sight. The sea might have been any sea by the look of it, but he knew it was the Mediterranean, that splendid enclosure which held all the world's history and half the happiest memories of his own life; of work and rest and battle, of aesthetic adventure, and of young love.

After breakfast he took a book to the lounge, not to his listening post in the panelled corner, but to an isolated chair in the centre, and read, undisturbed. He must get out of that haunted cabin, he thought; but not yet; later, in his own time.

Presently he rose and began once more to walk the decks. They were thronged now. All the passengers seemed to be there, occupied as before in reading, knitting, dozing, or strolling like himself, but that morning he found a kind of paschal novelty in the scene and rejoiced in it until he was rudely disturbed in his benevolence.

The passengers, too, seemed aware of change. They must all at one time or another in the last few days have caught sight of Mr Pinfold. Now, however, it was as though he were a noteworthy, unaccompanied female, newly appearing in the evening promenade of some stagnant South American town. He had been witness of such an event on many a dusty plaza; he had seen the sickly faces of the men brighten, their lassitude take sudden life; he had observed the little flourishes of seedy dandyism; he had heard the jungle whistles and, without fully understanding them, the frank, anatomical appraisals; had seen the sly following and pinching of the unwary tourist. In just that way Mr Pinfold, wherever he went that day, found himself to be such a cynosure; everyone was talking about him, loudly and unashamedly, but not in his praise.

'That's Gilbert Pinfold, the writer.'

'That common little man? It can't be.'

'Have you read his books? He has a very *peculiar* sense of humour, you know.'

'He is very peculiar altogether. His hair is very long.'

'He's wearing lipstick.'

'He's painted up to the eyes.'

'But he's so shabby. I thought people like that were always smart.'

'There are different types of homosexual, you know. What are called "poufs" and "nancies" – that is the dressy kind. Then there are the others they call "butch". I read a book about it. Pinfold is a "butch".'

That was the first conversation Mr Pinfold overheard. He stopped, turned, and tried to stare out of countenance the little group of middle-aged women who were speaking. One of them smiled at him and then, turning, said: 'I believe he's trying to get to know us.'

'How disgusting.'

Mr Pinfold walked on but wherever he went he was the topic.

'. . . Lord of the Manor of Lychpole.'

'Anyone can be that. It's often a title that goes with some tumbledown farmhouse these days.'

'Oh, Pinfold lives in great style I can tell you. Footmen in livery.'

'I can guess what he does with the footmen.'

'Not any more. He's been impotent for years, you know. That's why he's always thinking of death.'

'Is he always thinking of death?'

'Yes. He'll commit suicide one of these days, you'll see.'

'I thought he was a Catholic. They aren't allowed to commit suicide, are they?'

'That wouldn't stop Pinfold. He doesn't really *believe* in

his religion, you know. He just pretends to because he thinks it aristocratic. It goes with being Lord of the Manor.'

'There's only one Lychpole in the world, he told the wireless man.'

'Only one Lychpole and Pinfold is its Lord . . . '

'. . . There he is, drunk again.'

'He looks ghastly.'

'A dying man, if ever I saw one.'

'Why doesn't he kill himself?'

'Give him time. He's doing his best. Drink and drugs. He daren't go to a doctor, of course, for fear he'd be put in a home.'

'Best place for him, I should have thought.'

'Best place for him would be over the side.'

'Rather a nuisance for poor Captain Steerforth.'

'It's a great nuisance for Captain Steerforth having him on board.'

'And at his own table.'

'That's being taken care of. Haven't you heard? There's going to be a petition.'

'. . . Yes, I've signed. Everyone has, I believe.'

'Except those actually at the table. The Scarfields wouldn't, or Glover.'

'I see it might be a little awkward for them.'

'It's a very well-worded petition.'

'Yes. The general did that. It makes no specific accusation, you see, that might be libellous. Simply: "*We the undersigned, for reasons which we are prepared to state in confidence, consider it to be an insult to us, as passengers in the* Caliban, *that Mr Gilbert Pinfold should sit at the Captain's table, a position of honour for which he is notoriously unsuitable.*" That's very neatly put.'

'. . . the Captain ought to lock him up. He has full authority.'

'But he hasn't actually *done* anything yet, on board.'

This was a pair of genial business men with whom and the Scarfields Mr Pinfold had spent half an hour one evening.

'For his own protection. It was a very near thing the other night that those boys didn't beat him up.'

'They were drunk.'

'They may get drunk again. It would be most unpleasant for everyone if there was a police court case.'

'Couldn't something be put in our petition about that?'

'It was discussed. The generals thought it could best be left to the interview. The Captain is bound to ask them to give their reasons.'

'Not in writing.'

'Exactly. They don't suggest putting him in the cell. Simply confining him to his cabin.'

'He probably has certain legal rights, having paid his fare, to his cabin and his meals.'

'But *not* to his meals at the Captain's table.'

'There you have the crux.'

'. . . No,' the Norwegian was saying, 'I did not sign anything. It is a British matter. All I know is that he is a fascist. I have heard him speak ill of democracy. We had a few such men in the time of Quisling. We knew what to do with them. But I will not mix in these British affairs.'

'I've got a photograph of him in a black shirt taken at one of those Albert Hall meetings before the war.'

'That might be useful.'

'He was up to his eyes in it. He'd have been locked up under 18B but he escaped by joining the army.'

'He did pretty badly there, I suppose?'

'*Very* badly. There was a scandal in Cairo that had to be hushed up when his brigade-major shot himself.'

'Blackmail?'

'The next best thing.'

'I see he's wearing the Guards tie.'

'He wears any kind of tie – old Etonian usually.'

'*Was* he ever at Eton?'

'He says he was,' said Glover.

'Don't you believe it. Board-school through and through.'

'Or at Oxford?'

'No, no. His whole account of his early life is a lie. No one had ever heard of him until a year or two ago. He's one of a lot of nasty people who crept into prominence during the war . . .'

'. . . I don't say he's an actual card-carrying member of the communist party, but he's certainly mixed up with them.'

'Most Jews are.'

'Exactly. And those "missing diplomats". They were friends of his.'

'He doesn't know enough to make it worth the Russians' while to take him to Moscow.'

'Even the Russians wouldn't want Pinfold.'

The most curious encounter of that morning was with Mrs Cockson and Mrs Benson. They were sitting as usual on the veranda of the deck-bar, each with her glass, and they were talking French with what seemed to Mr Pinfold, who spoke the language clumsily, pure accent and idiom. Mrs Cockson said: '*Ce Monsieur Pinfold essaye toujours de pénétrer chez moi, et il a essayé de se faire présenter à moi par plusieurs de mes amis. Naturellement j'ai refusé.*'

'*Connaissez-vous un seul de ses amis? Il me semble qu'il a des relations très ordinaires.*'

'*On peut toujours se tromper dans le premier temps sur une relation étrangère. On a fini par s'apercevoir à Paris qu'il n'est pas de notre société . . .*'

It was a put-up job, Mr Pinfold decided. People did not normally behave in this way.

When Mr Pinfold first joined Bellamy's there was an old earl who had sat alone all day and every day in the corner of the stairs wearing an odd, hard hat and talking loudly to himself. He had one theme, the passing procession of his fellow members. Sometimes he dozed, but in his long waking hours he maintained a running commentary – 'That fellow's chin is too big; dreadful-looking fellow. Never saw him before. Who let him in? . . . Pick your feet up, you. Wearing the carpets out . . . Dreadfully fat young Crambo's getting. Don't eat, don't drink, it's just he's hard up. Nothing fattens a man like getting hard up . . . Poor old Nailsworth, his mother was a whore, so's his wife. They say his daughter's going the same way . . .' and so on.

In the broad tolerance of Bellamy's this eccentric had been accepted quite fondly. He was dead many years now. It was not conceivable, Mr Pinfold thought, that all the passengers in the *Caliban* should suddenly have become similarly afflicted. This chatter was designed to be overheard. It was a put-up job. It was in fact the generals' subtle plan, substituted for the adolescent violence of their young.

Twenty-five years ago or more Mr Pinfold, who was in love with one of them, used to frequent a house full of bright, cruel girls who spoke their own thieves' slang and played their own games. One of these games was a trick from the school-room polished for drawing-room use. When a stranger came among them, they would all – if the mood took them – put out their tongues at him or her; all, that is to say, except those in his immediate line of sight. As he turned his head, one group of tongues popped in, another popped out. Those girls were adept in dialogue. They had rigid self-control. They never giggled. Those who spoke to the stranger assumed an un-natural sweetness. The aim was to make him catch another with her tongue out. It was a comic performance – the turning head, the flickering, crimson stabs, the tender smiles turning to sudden grimaces, the artificiality of the conversation which soon engendered an unidentifiable discomfort in the most insensitive visitor, made him feel that somehow he was mak-ing a fool of himself, made him look at his trouser buttons, at his face in the glass to see whether there was something ridicul-ous in his appearance.

Some sort of game as this, enormously coarsened, must, Mr Pinfold supposed, have been devised by the passengers in the *Caliban* for their amusement and his discomfort. Well, he was not going to give them the satisfaction of taking notice of it. He no longer glanced to see who was speaking.

'. . . His mother sold her few little pieces of jewellery, you know, to pay his debts . . .'

'. . . Were his books ever any good?'

'Never *good*. His earlier ones weren't quite as bad as his latest. He's written out.'

'He's tried every literary trick. He's finished now and he knows it.'

'I suppose he's made a lot of money?'

'Not as much as he pretends. And he's spent every penny. His debts are enormous.'

'And of course they'll catch him for income-tax soon.'

'Oh, yes. He's been putting in false returns for years.

They're investigating him now. They don't hurry. They always get their man in the end.'

'They'll get Pinfold.'

'He'll have to sell Lychpole.'

'His children will go to the board-school.'

'Just as he did himself.'

'No more champagne for Pinfold.'

'No more cigars.'

'I suppose his wife will leave him?'

'Naturally. No home for her. Her family will take her in.'

'But not Pinfold.'

'No. Not Pinfold . . . '

Mr Pinfold would not give ground. There must be no appearance of defeat. But in his own time, when he had sauntered long enough, he retired to his cabin.

'Gilbert,' said Margaret. 'Gilbert. Why don't you speak to me? You passed quite close to me on deck and you never looked at me. *I* haven't offended you, have I? You know it isn't me who's saying all these beastly things, don't you? Answer me, Gilbert. I can hear you.'

So Mr Pinfold, not uttering the words but pronouncing them in his mind, said: 'Where are you? I don't even know you by sight. Why don't we meet, now? Come and have a cocktail with me.'

'Oh, Gilbert, darling, you know that's not possible. The *Rules*.'

'What rules? Whose? Do you mean your father won't let you?'

'No, Gilbert, not *his* rules, *the* Rules. Don't you understand? It's against *the Rules* for us to meet. I can talk to you now and then but we must never meet.'

'What do you look like?'

'I mustn't tell you that. You must find out for yourself. That's one of the Rules.'

'You talk as though we were playing some kind of game.'

'That's all we are doing – playing a kind of game. I must go now. But there's one thing I'd like to say.'

'Well?'

'You won't be offended?'

'I don't expect so.'

'Are you sure, darling?'

'What is it?'

'Shall I tell you? Dare I? You won't be offended? Well . . .' Margaret paused and then in a thrilling whisper said: '*Get your hair cut.*'

'Well, I'll be damned,' said Mr Pinfold; but Margaret was gone and did not hear him.

He looked in the glass. Yes, his hair was rather long. He would get it cut. Then he pondered the new problem: how had Margaret heard his soundless words? That could not be explained on any theory of frayed and crossed wires. As he considered the matter Margaret briefly returned to say: 'Not *wires*, darling. *Wireless,*' and then was gone again.

That perhaps should have given him the clue he sought; should have dispelled the mystery that enveloped him. He would learn in good time; at that moment Mr Pinfold was baffled, almost stupefied, by the occurrences of the morning and he went down to luncheon at the summons of the gong thinking vaguely in terms of telepathy, a subject on which he was ill-informed.

At the table he tackled Glover at once on a question that vexed him. 'I was not at Eton,' he said suddenly, with a challenge in his tone.

'Nor was I,' said Glover. 'Marlborough.'

'I never said I was at Eton,' Mr Pinfold insisted.

'No. Why should you, I mean, if you weren't?'

'It is a school for which I have every respect, but I was not there myself.' Then he turned across to the table to the Norwegian. 'I never wore a black shirt in the Albert Hall.'

'No?' said the Norwegian, interested but uncomprehending.

'I had every sympathy with Franco during the Civil War.'

'Yes? It is so long ago I have rather forgotten what it was all about. In my country we did not pay so much attention as the French and some other nations.'

'I never had the smallest sympathy with Hitler.'

'No, I suppose not.'

'Once I had hopes of Mussolini. But I was never connected with Mosley.'

'Mosley? What is that?'

'Please, please,' cried pretty Mrs Scarfield, 'don't let's get on to politics.'

For the rest of the meal Mr Pinfold sat silent.

Later he went to the barber's shop and from there to his listening post in the empty lounge. He saw the ship's surgeon pass the windows. He was on his way, evidently, to the Captain's cabin for almost immediately Mr Pinfold heard him say: '. . . I thought I ought to report it to you, skipper.'

'Where was he last seen?'

'In the barber's shop. After that he completely disappeared. He's not in his cabin.'

'Why should he have gone overboard?'

'I've had my eye on him ever since we sailed. Haven't you noticed anything odd about him?'

'I've noticed he drinks.'

'Yes, he's a typical alcoholic. Several of the passengers asked me to look him over, but I can't you know, unless he calls me in or unless he does something violent. Now they're all saying he's jumped overboard.'

'I'm not going to stop the ship and put out a boat simply because a passenger isn't in his cabin. He's probably in some-one else's cabin with one of my female passengers doing you know what.'

'Yes, that's the most likely explanation.'

'Is there anything the matter with him apart from the bottle?'

'Nothing a day's hard work wouldn't cure. The best thing for him would be to be put swabbing decks for a week...'

And after that the ship, like an aviary, was noisy with calls and chatter.

'... He can't be found.'

'... Overboard.'

'... No one's seen him since he left the barber ...'

'... The Captain thinks he's got a woman somewhere ...'

Very wearily Mr Pinfold tried to shut his mind to these distractions and to read his book. Presently the note changed. 'It's all right, he's found.'

'... False alarm.'

'... Pinfold's found.'

'I'm glad of that,' said the general gravely. 'I was afraid we might have gone too far.'

And the rest was silence.

The cutting of Mr Pinfold's hair fomented relations with Margaret. She prattled off and on all that afternoon and evening, gloating fondly over the change in Mr Pinfold's appearance; he looked younger, she said, smarter, altogether more lovable. Gazing long and earnestly into his looking-glass, turning his head this way and that, Mr Pinfold saw nothing very different from what he was used to, nothing to justify this enthusiasm. Margaret's gratification, he surmised, sprang less from his enhanced beauty than from the evidence he had given of his trust in her.

Interspersed with her praises there was an occasional hint of some deeper significance: '. . . Think, Gilbert. *Barber's shop*. Doesn't that tell you anything?'

'No. Should it?'

'It's the *clue*, Gilbert. It's what you most want to know, what you *must* know.'

'Well, tell me.'

'I can't do that, darling. It's against the *Rules*. But I can hint. *Barber's shop*, Gilbert. What do barbers do beside cutting hair?'

'They try and sell one hairwash.'

'No. No.'

'They make conversation. They massage the scalp. They iron moustaches. They sometimes, I believe, cut people's corns.'

'Oh, Gilbert, something much simpler. Think, darling. Sh . . . Sh . . . '

'Shave?'

'Got it.'

'But I shaved this morning. You're not asking me to shave again?'

'Oh, Gilbert, I think you're sweet. Is your chin a little bit rough, darling? How long after you shave does it get rough again? I *think* I should like it rough . . . ' And she was off again on her galloping declaration of love.

More than once Mr Pinfold – or rather a fanciful image of him derived from his books – had been the object of adolescent infatuation. Margaret's fervent, naïve tones reminded him of the letters which used to come two a day usually for periods of a week or ten days, written in bed probably. They were confidences and avowals of love, bearing no address; asking no reciprocation or sign of recognition; the series ending as abruptly as it had begun. As a rule, he read none after the first, but here on the hostile *Caliban*, these guileless words uttered in Margert's sweet, breathless tones fell softly on Mr Pinfold's ear and he listened complacently. Indeed he began to relish these moments of unction which compensated for much of the ignorant abuse. That morning he had determined to change his cabin. That evening he was loth to cut himself off from this warm spring.

But night brought a change.

Mr Pinfold did not dress or dine. He was very weary and he sat alone on deck until the passengers began to come up from dinner. Then he went to his cabin and for the first time for three days put on pyjamas, said his prayers, got into bed, turned off the light, composed himself for sleep, and slept.

He was awakened by Margaret's mother.

'Mr Pinfold. Mr Pinfold. Surely you haven't gone to sleep? Everyone is in bed now. Surely you haven't forgotten your promise to Margaret?'

'Mother, he didn't make any promise.' Margaret's voice was tearful and strained, almost hysterical. 'Not really. Not really what you could call a *promise*. Don't you see how awful it is for *me*, if you upset him now? He never *promised*.'

'When I was young, dear, any man would be proud of a pretty girl taking notice of him. He wouldn't try and get out of it by pretending to be asleep.'

'I asked for it. I expect I bore him. He's a man of the world. He's had hundreds of other girls, all sorts of horrible, fashionable, vicious old hags in London and Paris and Rome and New York. Why should he look at *me*? But I *do* love him so,' and in her anguish she uttered the whimper which Mr Pinfold had heard before in this ship on other lips.

'Don't cry, my dear. Mother will talk to him.'

'Please, *please* not, Mother. I forbid you to interfere.'

'"Forbid" isn't a very nice word, is it, dear? You leave it to me. I'll talk to him. Mr Pinfold. *Gilbert*. Wake up. Margaret's got something to say to you. He's awake now, dear, I know. Just tell her you're awake and listening, Gilbert.'

'I'm awake and listening,' said Mr Pinfold.

'All right then, hold on' – she was like a telephone operator, Mr Pinfold thought – 'Margaret's going to speak to you. Come along, Margaret, speak up.'

'I can't, Mother, I can't.'

'You see, Gilbert, you've upset her. Tell her you love her. You do love her, don't you?'

'But I've never met her,' said Mr Pinfold desperately. 'I'm sure she's a delightful girl, but I've never set eyes on her.'

'Oh, Gilbert, Gilbert, that's not a very gallant thing to say, is it? Not really like you, not like the *real* you. You just pretend to be hard and worldly, don't you? and you can't blame people if they take you at your own estimate. Everyone in the ship you know, has been saying the most odious things about you. But I know better. Margaret wants to come and say good night to you, Gilbert, but she's not sure you really love her. Just tell Mimi you love her, Gilbert.'

'I can't, I don't,' said Mr Pinfold. 'I'm sure your daughter is a most charming girl. It so happens I have never met her. It also happens that I have a wife. I love *her*.'

'Oh, Gilbert, what a very middle-class thing to say!'

'He doesn't love me,' wailed Margaret. 'He doesn't love me any more.'

'Gilbert, Gilbert, you're breaking my little girl's heart.'

Mr Pinfold was exasperated.

'I'm going to sleep now,' he said. 'Good night.'

'Margaret's coming to see you.'

'Oh, shut up, you old bitch,' said Mr Pinfold.

He should not have said it. The moment the words crossed his lips – or, rather, his mind – he knew it was not the right thing to say. The whole sturdy ship seemed to tremble with shock. There was a single piteous wail from Margaret, from her mother an inarticulate but plainly audible hiss of outrage, an attempt at bluster from the son: 'My God, Peinfold, you'll pay for that. If you think you can talk to my mother like . . . ' And then, most unexpectedly came a hearty chuckle from the general.

'Upon my soul, my dear, he called you an old bitch. Good for Peinfold. That's something I've been longing to say to you for thirty years. You *are* an old bitch, you know, a thorough old bitch. Now perhaps you'll allow *me* to handle the situation. Clear out, the lot of you. I want to talk to my daughter. Come here, Meg, Peg o' my heart, my little Mimi.' The voices became thick, the diction strangely Celtic as sentiment overpowered the military man. 'You'll not be my little Mimi ever again, any more after tonight and I'll not forget it. You're a woman now and you've set your heart on a man as a woman should. The choice is yours, not mine. He's old for you, but there's good in that. Many a young couple spend a wretched fortnight together through not knowing how to set about what has to be done. And an old man can show you better than a young one. He'll be gentler and kinder and cleaner; and then, when the right time comes you in your turn can teach a younger man – and that's how the art of love is learned and the breed survives. I'd like dearly to be the one myself to teach you, but you've made your own choice and who's to grudge it you?'

'But, Father, he doesn't love me. He said not.'

'Fiddlesticks. You're as pretty a girl as he'll meet in a twelvemonth. There's certainly no one in this ship to touch you and if he's the man I think, he'll be feeling the need of an armful by now. Go in and get him, lass. How do you think your mother got me? Not by waiting to be asked, I can tell you. She was a soldier's daughter. She always rode straight at her fences. She rode straight at me, I can tell you. Don't forget you're a soldier's daughter too. If you want this fellow Pinfold, go in and take him. But for God's sake come on parade looking like a soldier. Get yourself cleaned up. Wash your face, brush your hair, take your clothes off.'

Margaret went obediently to her cabin. There she was joined by her friend, several friends, it seemed, a whole choir of bridesmaids who chanted an epithalamium as they disrobed her and tired her hair.

Mr Pinfold listened with conflicting resentment and fascination. He was a man accustomed to his own preferences and decisions. It seemed to him that Margaret's parents were being officious and presumptuous, were making altogether too free with his passions. He had never, even in his bachelor days, been a strenuous philanderer. Abroad, especially in remote places, he used to patronize brothels with the curiosity of a traveller who sought to taste all flavours of the exotic. In England he was rather constant and rather romantic in his affections. Since marriage he had been faithful to his wife. He had, since his acceptance of the laws of the Church, developed what approximated to a virtuous disposition; a reluctance to commit deliberate grave sins, which was independent of the fear of Hell; he had assumed a personality to which such specifically forbidden actions were inappropriate. And yet amorous expectations began to stir in Mr Pinfold. That acquired restraint and dignity of his had suffered some hard knocking-

about during the last few days. Margaret's visit was exciting.
He started to plan her reception.

The cabin with its two narrow bunks was ill-designed for
such purposes. He began by tidying it, putting away his
clothes and straightening the bed. He succeeded only in
making it look unoccupied. She would enter by that door. She
must not find him reclining like a pasha. He must be on his feet.
There was one chair only. Should he offer it to her? Somehow
he must dispose her, supine, on the bunk. But how to get her
there silently and gracefully. How to shift her? Was she
portable? He wished that he knew her dimensions.

He took off his pyjamas and hung them in his cupboard,
put on his dressing-gown, and sat in the chair facing the door,
waiting, while the folk-ritual of Margaret's preparations filled
the cabin with music. As he waited his mood changed. Doubt
and dismay intruded on his loving fancies. What on earth was
he up to? What was he letting himself in for? He thought
with disgust of Clutton-Cornforth and his tedious succession
of joyless, purposeful seductions. He thought of his own en-
feebled condition. 'Feeling the need of an armful' indeed!
Would he be able to sustain his interest during all the patient
exploration required of him? Then, as he gazed at the tidy
bunk, he filled it with delicate, shrinking, yielding, yearning
nudity, with a nymph by Boucher or Fragonard, and his mood
changed again. Let her come. Let her come speedily. He was
strongly armed for the encounter.

But Margaret did not hurry. The attendant virgins
completed their services. She was inspected by both
parents.

'Oh my darling, my own. You're so young. Are you sure?
Are you quite sure you love him. You can always turn back.
It's not too late. I shall never see you again as I am seeing you
now, my innocent daughter.'

'Yes, mother, I love him.'

'Be kind to her, Gilbert. You have not been kind to me. You used an expression to me that I never expected to hear on a man's lips. I meant never to speak to you again. But this is no moment for pride. My daughter's happiness is in your hands. Treat her *husbandly*. I'm entrusting something very precious to you . . .'

And the general: 'That's my beauty. Go and take what's coming to you. Listen, my Peg, you know what you're in for, don't you?'

'Yes, father, I think so.'

'It's always a surprise. You may think you know it all on paper, but like everything else in life it's never quite what you expect when it comes to action. There's no going back now. Come and see me when it's all over. I'll be waiting up to hear the report. In you go, bless you.'

But still the girl delayed.

'Gilbert. Gilbert. Do you want me?' she asked. 'Really and truly?'

'Yes, of course, come along.'

'Say something sweet to me.'

'I'll be sweet enough when you get here.'

'Come and fetch me.'

'Where are you?'

'Here. Just outside your cabin.'

'Well, come along in. I've left the door open.'

'I can't. I can't. You've got to come and fetch me.'

'Oh, don't be such a little ass. I've been sitting here for goodness knows how long. Come in if you're coming. If you're not, I want to go back to bed.'

At this Margaret broke into weeping and her mother said: 'Gilbert, that wasn't kind. It wasn't like you. You love her. She loves you. Can't you understand? A young girl; the first time; woo her, Gilbert, coax her. She's a little wild, woodland thing.'

'What the hell's going on?' asked the general. 'You ought to be in position by now. Haven't had a Sitrep. Isn't the girl over the Start Line?'

'Oh, Father, I can't. I *can't*. I thought I could, but I *can't*.'

'Something's gone wrong, Pinfold. Find out. Send out patrols.'

'Go and find her, Gilbert. Lure her in, tenderly, *husbandly*. She's just there waiting for you.'

Rather crossly Mr Pinfold strode into the empty corridor. He could hear Glover snoring. He could hear Margaret weeping quite close to him. He looked in the bathroom; not there. He looked round each corner, up and down the stairs; not there. He even looked in the lavatories, men's and women's; not there. Still the sobbing continued piteously. He returned to his cabin, fixed the door open on its hook and drew the curtain. He was overcome by weariness and boredom.

'I'm sorry, Margaret,' he said, 'I'm too old to start playing hide and seek with schoolgirls. If you want to come to bed with me, you'll have to come and join me there.'

He put on his pyjamas and lay down, pulling the blankets up to his chin. Presently he stretched out his arm and turned off the light. Then the passage light was disturbing. He shut the door. He rolled over on his side and lay between sleep and waking. Just as he was falling into unconsciousness he heard his door open and quickly shut. He opened his eyes too late to see the momentary gleam of light from the corridor. He heard slippered feet scurrying away and Margaret's despairing wail.

'I did go to him. I did. I did. I did. And when I got there he was lying in the dark snoring.'

'Oh, my Margaret, my daughter. You should never have gone. It was all your father's fault.'

'Sorry about that, Peg,' said the general. 'False appreciation.'

The last voice Mr Pinfold heard before he fell asleep was Goneril's: 'Snoring? Shamming. Gilbert knew he wasn't up to it. He's impotent, aren't you, Gilbert? Aren't you?'

'It was Glover snoring,' said Mr Pinfold, but nobody seemed to hear him.

7

THE VILLAINS UNMASKED –
BUT NOT FOILED

MR PINFOLD did not sleep for very long. He awoke as usual when the men began washing the deck overhead and he woke with the firm resolution of changing his cabin that day. His bond with Margaret was severed. He wished to be rid of the whole set of them and to sleep in peace in a cabin free of electrical freaks. He resolved, too, to move from the Captain's table. He had never wished to sit there. Anyone who coveted the place was welcome to it. Mr Pinfold was going to be strictly private for the rest of the voyage.

This resolution was confirmed by the last of the many communications that had come to him in that cabin.

Shortly before the breakfast hour, the device brought him into contact with what he might have supposed would be its most natural source, the wireless office; he found himself listening not as before to the normal traffic of the ship, but to the conversation of the wireless operator, and this man was entertaining a party of early-risers, the bright young people, by reading to them the text of Mr Pinfold's own messages.

'"*Everyone in ship most helpful. Love. Gilbert.*"'

'That's a good one.'

'Everyone?'

'I wonder if poor Gilbert thinks that now?'

'*Love.* Love from Gilbert. That's funny.'

'Show us some more.'

'Strictly speaking, you know, I oughtn't to. They're supposed to be confidential.'

'Oh, come off it, Sparks.'

'Well, this is rather rich. "*Entirely cured. All love.*"'

'Cured? Ha. Ha.'

'*Entirely* cured.'

'Our Gilbert *entirely cured*! Yes, that's delicious. Oh, Sparks, read us some more.'

'I've never known a chap spend so much on radiograms. They're mostly just about money and often he was so drunk I couldn't read what he'd written. There are an awful lot just refusing invitations. Oh, here's a good series. "*Kindly arrange immediate luxury private bath. Kindly investigate wanton inefficiency your office.*" He sent out dozens of those.'

'Thank God for our Gilbert. What should we do without him?'

'Was his luxury private bath inefficient?'

'"Wanton" is good coming from Gilbert. Does he wanton in his bath?'

To Mr Pinfold this little scene was different in kind from the earlier annoyances. The bright young people had gone too far. It was one thing to play practical jokes on him; it was something quite else to read confidential messages. They had put themselves outside the law. Mr Pinfold left his cabin for the dining-saloon with set purpose. He would put them on a charge.

He met the Captain making his morning round.

'Captain Steerforth, may I speak to you for a moment?'

'Surely.' The Captain paused.

'In your cabin?'

'Yes, if you want to. I shall be through in ten minutes. Come up then. Or is it very urgent?'

'It can wait ten minutes.'

Mr Pinfold climbed to the cabin behind the bridge. Few

personal additions embellished the solid ship's furniture. There were family photographs in leather frames; an etching of an English Cathedral on the panelled wall which might have been the Captain's property or the company's; some pipes in a rack. Mr Pinfold could not imagine this place the scene of orgy, outrage, or plot.

Presently the Captain returned.

'Well, sir, and what can I do for you?'

'First, I want to know whether radiograms sent from your ship are confidential documents?'

'I'm sorry. I'm afraid I don't understand you.'

'Captain Steerforth, since I came on board I have sent out a large number of messages of an entirely private character. This morning, early, there were a group of passengers reading them aloud in the wireless-room.'

'Well, we can easily get the facts about that. How many of these radiograms were there?'

'I don't know exactly. About a dozen.'

'And when did you send them?'

'At various times during the early days of the voyage.'

Captain Steerforth looked perplexed. 'This is only our fifth day out, you know,' he said.

'Oh,' said Mr Pinfold, disconcerted, 'are you quite sure?'

'Yes, of course I'm sure.'

'It seems longer.'

'Well, come along to the office and we'll look into the matter.'

The wireless-room was only two doors from the Captain's cabin.

'This is Mr Pinfold, a passenger.'

'Yes, sir. We've seen him before.'

'He wants to inquire about some radiograms he sent.'

'We can easily check on that, sir. We've had practically no

private traffic!' He opened a file at his side and said: 'Yes. Here we are. The day before yesterday. It went out within an hour of being handed in.'

He showed Mr Pinfold's holograph: *Entirely cured. All love.*

'But the others?' said Mr Pinfold, bewildered.

'There were no others, sir.'

'A dozen or more.'

'Only this one. I should know, I can assure you.'

'There was one I sent at Liverpool, the evening I came on board.'

'That would have gone by Post Office Telegraph, sir.'

'And you wouldn't have a copy here?'

'No, sir.'

'Then how,' said Mr Pinfold, 'was it possible for a group of passengers to read it aloud in this office at eight o'clock this morning?'

'Quite impossible,' said the wireless operator. 'I was on duty myself at that time. There were no passengers here.'

He and the Captain exchanged glances.

'Does that satisfy all your questions, Mr Pinfold?' asked the Captain.

'Not quite. May I come back to your cabin?'

'If you wish it.'

When they were seated Mr Pinfold said: 'Captain Steerforth, I am the victim of a practical joke.'

'Something of the sort, it seems,' said the Captain.

'Not for the first time. Ever since I came on board this ship – you say it has only been five days?'

'Four actually.'

'Ever since I came on board, I have been the victim of hoaxes and threats. Mind you I am not making any accusation. I don't know the names of these people. I don't even know what they look like. I am *not* asking for an official investigation

– yet. What I do know is that the leaders comprise a family of four.'

'I don't believe we have any families on board,' said the Captain, taking the passenger list off his desk, 'except the Angels. I hardly think they're the sort of people to play practical jokes on anyone. A very quiet family.'

'There are several people travelling who aren't on that list.'

'No one, I assure you.'

'Fosker for one.'

Captain Steerforth turned the pages. 'No,' he said. 'No Fosker.'

'And that little dark man who used to sit alone in the dining-saloon.'

'Him? I know him well. He often travels with us. Mr Murdoch – here he is on the list.'

Baffled, Mr Pinfold turned to another course suggested by Mr Murdoch's solitary meals.

'Another thing, Captain. I greatly appreciate the honour of being invited to sit at your table in the dining-saloon. But the truth is I'm not fit for human society, just at the moment. I've been taking some grey pills – pretty strong stuff, for rheumatism, you know. I'm really better alone. So if you won't think it rude . . .'

'Sit where you like, Mr Pinfold. Just tell the chief steward.'

'Please understand I am not going because of any pressure from outside. It is simply that I am not well.'

'I quite understand, Mr Pinfold.'

'I reserve the right to return if I feel better.'

'Please sit exactly where you like, Mr Pinfold. Is that all you wanted to say?'

'No. There's another thing. The cabin I'm in. You ought to get the wiring seen to. I don't know whether you know it, but I can often hear anything that's being said up here, on the bridge and in other parts of the ship.'

'I didn't know,' said Captain Steerforth. 'That is most unusual.'

'They've used this defect in their practical jokes. It's most disturbing. I should like to change cabins.'

'That should be easy. We have two or three vacant. If you'll tell the purser . . . Is *that* everything, Mr Pinfold?'

'Yes,' said Mr Pinfold. 'Thank you very much. I am most grateful to you. And you *do* understand about my changing tables? You don't think it rude?'

'No offence whatever, Mr Pinfold. Good morning.'

Mr Pinfold left the cabin far from content with his interview. It seemed to him that he had said too much or too little. But he had achieved certain limited objectives and he set about his business with the purser and chief steward with alacrity. He was given the very table where Mr Murdoch had sat. Of several cabins he chose a small one near the veranda-bar which gave immediate access to the promenade-deck. Here, he was sure, he would be safe from physical attack.

He returned to his old cabin to direct the removal of his possessions. The voices began at once but he was very busy with the English-speaking steward and did not listen until he had seen his clothes and belongings packed and carried away. Then briefly he surveyed the scene of his suffering and lent them his ears. He was gratified to find that, however incomplete it looked to him, his morning's work had dismayed his enemies.

'Dirty little sneak' – there was a note of fear in Goneril's hatred that morning – 'what have you been saying to the Captain? We'll get even with you. Have you forgotten the three-eight rhythm? Did you tell him our names? Did you? Did you?'

Margaret's brother was positively conciliatory: 'Look here, Gilbert, old boy, we don't want to bring other people into our business, do we? We can settle it between ourselves, can't we, Gilbert?'

Margaret was reproachful; not because of the drama of the night; all that storm of emotion seemed to have passed leaving no more trace than thunder clouds in the blue of summer. Indeed in all their subsequent acquaintance she never mentioned that fiasco; she chid him instead gently for his visit to the Captain. 'It's *against the Rules*, darling, don't you see? We *must* all play by the Rules.'

'I'm not playing at all.'

'Oh yes, darling, you are. We all are. We can't help ourselves. And it's a Rule that no one else must be told. If there's anything you don't understand, ask me.'

Poor waif, Mr Pinfold thought, she has kept bad company and been corrupted. After the embarrassments of the night Margaret had forfeited his trust, but he loved her a little and felt it unmannerly to be leaving her flat, as he planned to do. It had proved easy to move out of their reach. They had confided too much, these aggressive young people, in their mechanical toy. And now he was breaking it.

'Margaret,' he said, 'I don't know anything about your rules and I am not playing any game with any of you. But I should like to see you. Come and join me on deck any time you like.'

'Darling, you know I long to. But I can't, can I? You do see, don't you?'

'No,' said Mr Pinfold, 'frankly I don't see. I leave it to you. I'm off now,' and he left the haunted cabin for the last time.

It was the social hour of noon when the sweepstake was paid, the cocktails ordered. From his new cabin, where his new steward was unpacking, he could hear the chatter from the bar. He stood alone thinking how smoothly he had made the transition.

He repeated to himself all that had been said in the Captain's cabin: '. . . *no families on board except the Angels?*' Angel. And suddenly Mr Pinfold understood, not everything, but the heart of the mystery. Angel, the quizzical man from the B.B.C. ' – *not wires, darling. Wireless*' – Angel, the man with the technical skill to use the defects of the *Caliban*'s communications, perhaps to cause them. Angel, the man with the beard – '*What do barbers do besides cut hair?*' – Angel, who had an aunt near Lychpole and could have heard from her the garbled gossip of the countryside. Angel who had 'half expected' Cedric Thorne to kill himself; Angel who bore a grudge for the poor figure he had cut at Lychpole and had found Mr Pinfold by chance alone and ill and defenceless, ripe for revenge. Angel was the villain, he and his sinister associate – mistress? colleague? – whom Mr Pinfold had dubbed 'Goneril'. And Angel had gone too far. He was afraid now that his superiors in London might get wind of his escapade. And they would, too; Mr Pinfold would see to that, when he returned to England. He might even write from the ship. If, as seemed probable, he was travelling on duty, the B.B.C. would have something to say to young Angel, bearded or shaven.

There were many passages in the story of the last few days that remained obscure under this new, bright light. Mr Pinfold felt as though he had come to the end of an ingenious, old-fashioned detective novel which he had read rather inattentively. He knew the villain now and began turning back the pages to observe the clues he had missed.

It was not the first time in the *Caliban* that noon had brought an illusion of shadowless commonplace.

The change of cabin was not the tactical triumph Mr Pinfold briefly supposed. He was like a commander whose attack 'hit air'. The post he had captured, which had seemed the key of the enemy's position, proved to be empty, a mere piece of deception masking an elaborate and strongly held system; the force he supposed routed was reinforced and ready for the counter-attack.

Mr Pinfold discovered, before he went down to his first lonely luncheon, that Angel's range of action was not limited to the original cabin and the corner of the lounge. From some mobile point of control he could speak, and listen in every part of the ship and in the following days Mr Pinfold, wherever he stood, could hear, could not keep himself from hearing, everything that was said in Angel's headquarters. Living and moving and eating now quite alone, barely nodding to Glover or Mrs Scarfield, Mr Pinfold listened and spoke only to his enemies and hour by hour, day by day, night by night, carefully assembled the intricate pieces of a plot altogether more modern and horrific than anything in the classic fictions of murder.

Mr Pinfold's change of cabin had momentarily disconcerted Angel and his staff (there were about half a dozen of them, male and female, all young, basically identical with the three-eight orchestra); moreover it seemed likely that the scare of the day before, when it was put about the ship that he had gone overboard, was genuine enough. At any rate Angel's first concern was that Mr Pinfold should be kept under continual observation. Immediate reports were made to headquarters of his every move. These reports were concise and factual.

'Gilbert has sat down at his table . . . He's reading the menu . . . He's ordering wine . . . He's ordered a plate of cold ham.' When he moved he was passed on to relays of observers.

'Gilbert coming up to main deck. Take over, B.'

'O.K., A. Gilbert now approaching door on port side, going out on to deck. Take over, C.'

'O.K., B. Gilbert walking the deck anti-clockwise. He's approaching the main door, starboard side. Over to you B.'

'He's sitting down with a book.'

'O.K., B. Stay on duty in the lounge. Report any move. I'll have you relieved at three.'

Mr Pinfold, looking from one to another of the occupants of the lounge, wondered which was B. Later it transpired that about half the passengers had been recruited by Angel for observation duties. They considered it an innocuous parlour game. Of the rest some knew nothing of what was afoot – this group included Glover and the Scarfields – others thought the whole thing silly. The inner circle manned the staff office where reports were collated and inquiries instigated. Every few hours a conference was held at which Angel collected and discussed the notes of his observers, drafted them into a coherent report and gave them to a girl to be typed. He maintained a rollicking good humour and zest.

'Great stuff. Splendid . . . My word, Gilbert's given himself away here . . . Most valuable . . . We could do with a little more detail on these points . . .'

Anything Mr Pinfold had said or done or thought, that day or in his past life, seemed significant. Angel was mocking, but appreciative. At intervals two older men – not the generals, but men more akin to them than to the boisterous youngsters – subjected Mr Pinfold to direct questioning. This inquisition, it appeared, was the essence of the enterprise. It was prosecuted whenever Mr Pinfold sat in the lounge or lay in his cabin, and so curious was he about the motives and mechanics of the thing that for the first twenty-four hours he, to some extent, collaborated. The inquisitors, it seemed, possessed a huge but incomplete and wildly inaccurate dossier covering the whole of Mr Pinfold's private life. It was their task to fill the gaps. In manner they were part barristers, part bureaucrats.

'Where were you in January 1929, Pinfold?'

'I really don't know.'

'Perhaps I can refresh your memory. I have here a letter from you written at Mena House Hotel, Cairo. Were you in Egypt in 1929?'

'Yes, I believe I was.'

'And what were you doing there?'

'Nothing.'

'Nothing? That won't do, Pinfold. I want a better answer than that.'

'I was just travelling.'

'Of course you were travelling. You could hardly get to Egypt without travelling, could you? I want the truth, Pinfold. *What were you doing* in Egypt in 1929?'

On another occasion: 'How many pairs of shoes do you possess?'

'I really don't know.'

'You *must* know. Would you say a dozen?'

'Yes, I dare say.'

'We have you down here as possessing ten.'

'Perhaps.'

'Then why did you tell me a dozen, Pinfold? He did say a dozen, didn't he?'

'Quite distinctly.'

'I don't like this, Pinfold. You have to be truthful. Only the truth can help you.'

Sometimes they turned to more immediate topics.

'On more than one occasion you have complained of suffering from the effects of some grey pills. Where did they come from?'

'My doctor.'

'Do you suppose he manufactured them himself?'

'No, I suppose not.'

'Well then, answer my question properly. Where did those pills come from?'

'I really don't know. Some chemist, I suppose.'

'Exactly. Would it surprise you to hear they came from Wilcox and Bredworth?'

'Not particularly.'

'*Not particularly*, Pinfold? I must warn you to be careful. Don't you know that Wilcox and Bredworth are one of the most respected firms in the country?'

'Yes.'

'And you accuse them of purveying dangerous drugs?'

'I expect they manufacture great quantities of poison.'

'You mean you accuse Wilcox and Bredworth of conspiring with your doctor to poison you?'

'Of course I don't.'

'Then what *do* you mean?'

Sometimes they made in their stern, precise voices accusations as fantastic as those of the hooligans and the gossips. They pressed him for information about the suicide of a staff-officer in the Middle East – a man who to the best of Mr Pinfold's knowledge had ended the war healthily and prosperously – which they attributed to Mr Pinfold's malice. They brought up the old charges of the eviction of Hill and of Mrs Pinfold senior's pauper's funeral. They examined him about a claim he had never made, to be the nephew of an Anglican bishop.

Once or twice during these days Angel organized a rag, but since Mr Pinfold could hear the preparations, he was not dismayed as he had been by the previous exercises.

Early one morning he heard Angel announce: 'We will

mount Operation Storm today,' and as soon as the ship came
to life and the passengers began their day, all conversation,
when they passed Mr Pinfold, or he them, was about a gale
warning. '. . . The Captain says we're coming right into it.'

'One of the worst storms he's ever known in the Mediterranean . . .'

The day was bright and calm. Mr Pinfold had no fear – if
anything he had rather a relish – for rough weather. After an
hour of this charade Angel called it off. 'No good,' he said,
'operation cancelled. Gilbert isn't scared.'

'He's a good sailor,' said Margaret.

'He doesn't mind missing his lunch,' said Goneril. 'The
food isn't good enough for him.'

'Operation Stock Exchange,' said Angel.

This performance was even more fatuous than its pre-
decessor. The method was the same, a series of conversations
designed for him to hear. The subject was a financial slump
which had suddenly thrown the stock-markets of the world
into chaos. As they sauntered past or sat over their knitting
the passengers dutifully recounted huge falls in the prices of
stocks and shares in the world capital cities, the suicide of
financiers, the closing of banks and corporations. They
quoted figures. They named the companies which had failed.
All this, even had he believed it, would have been of very
remote interest to Mr Pinfold.

'They say Mr Pinfold's fortune is entirely wiped out,' said
Mrs Benson to Mrs Cockson (these ladies had now resumed
their mother tongue).

Mr Pinfold had no fortune. He owned a few fields, a few
pictures, a few valuable books, his own copyrights. At the bank
he had a small overdraft. He had never in his life put out a
penny at interest. The rudimentary technicalities of finance
were Greek to him. It was very odd, he thought, that these

people could go to so much trouble to investigate his affairs and know so little about them.

'Operation cancelled,' announced Angel at length.

'What went wrong?'

'I wish I knew. Gilbert is no longer responding to treatment. We had him on the run in the early days. Now he seems punch-drunk.'

'He's in a sort of daze.'

'He's not sleeping enough.'

This was indeed true. Since he had finished his sleeping-draught Mr Pinfold had seldom had more than an hour at a time of uneasy dozing. The nights were a bad time for him. He would sit in the lounge, alone in his dinner jacket, observing his fellow passengers, distracted a little by their activities from the voice of his enemies, trying to decide which were his friends, which were neutral, until the last of them had gone below and the lights were turned down. Then, knowing what to expect, he would go to his cabin and undress. He had given up any attempt at saying his prayers; the familiar, hallowed words provoked a storm of blasphemous parody from Goneril.

He lay down expecting little rest. Angel had in his headquarters an electric instrument which showed Mr Pinfold's precise state of consciousness. It consisted, Mr Pinfold surmised, of a glass tube containing two parallel lines of red light which continually drew together or moved apart like telegraph wires seen from a train. They approached one another as he grew drowsy and, when he fell asleep, crossed. A duty officer followed their fluctuations.

'... Wide awake ... now he's getting sleepy ... they're almost touching ... a single line ... they're going to cross ... no, wide awake again ...' And when he awoke after his brief spells of insensibility, his first sensation was always the voice of the observer: 'Gilbert's awake again. Fifty-one minutes.'

'That's better than the time before.'

'But it isn't enough.'

One night they tried to soothe him by playing a record specially made by Swiss scientists for the purpose. These savants had decided from experiments made in a sanatorium for neurotic industrial workers that the most soporific noises were those of a factory. Mr Pinfold's cabin resounded to the roar and clang of machinery.

'You bloody fools,' he cried in exasperation, '*I'm* not a factory worker. You're driving me mad.'

'No, no, Gilbert, you *are* mad already,' said the duty-officer. 'We're driving you insane.'

The hubbub continued until Angel came on his round of inspection.

'Gilbert not asleep yet? Let me see the log. "*0312 hours. You bloody fools, I'm not a factory worker.*" Well nor he is. "*You're driving me mad.*" I believe we are. Turn off that record. Give him something rural.'

From then for a long time nightingales sang to Mr Pinfold but still he did not sleep. He stepped out on deck and leaned on the rail.

'Go on, Gilbert. Jump. In you go,' said Goneril. Mr Pinfold did not feel the smallest temptation to obey. 'Water-funk.'

'I know all about that actor, you know,' said Mr Pinfold. 'The one who was a friend of Angel's and hanged himself in his dressing-room.'

This was the first time that he disclosed his knowledge of Angel's identity. The effect was immediate. All Angel's assumed good humour was dispelled. 'Why do you call me Angel?' he asked fiercely. 'What the devil do you mean by it?'

'It's your name. I know exactly what you are doing for the B.B.C.' – this was bluff – 'I know exactly what you did to Cedric Thorne. I know exactly what you are trying to do to me.'

'Liar. You don't know anything.'

'Liar,' said Goneril.

'I told you,' said Margaret, 'Gilbert's no fool.'

Silence fell on the headquarters. Mr Pinfold returned to his bunk, lay down, and slept until the steward came in with his tea. Angel spoke to him at once. He was in a chastened mood. 'Look here, Gilbert, you've got us all wrong. What we're doing is nothing to do with the B.B.C. It's a private enterprise entirely. And as for Cedric – that wasn't our fault. He came to us too late. We did everything we could for him. He was a hopeless case. Why don't you answer? Can't you hear me, Gilbert? Why don't you answer?'

Mr Pinfold held his peace. He was getting near to a full explanation.

Mr Pinfold was never able to give a completely coherent account either to himself or to anyone else of how he finally unravelled the mystery. He heard so much, directly and indirectly; he reasoned so closely; he followed so many false clues and reached so many absurd conclusions; but at length he was satisfied that he knew the truth. He then sat down and wrote about it at length to his wife.

Darling,

As I said in my telegram I am quite cured of my aches and pains. In that way the trip has been a success but this has not proved a happy ship and I have decided to get off at Port Said and go on by aeroplane.

Do you remember the tick with a beard who came to Lychpole from the B.B.C. He is on board with a team bound for Aden. They are going to make recordings of Arab dance music. The tick is called Angel. He has shaved his beard. That is why I didn't spot him at first. He has some of his family with him – rather a nice sister – travelling I suppose for pleasure. They seem to be cousins of a lot of our neighbours. You might inquire. These B.B.C. people have made themselves a great nuisance to me on board. They have got a lot of apparatus with them, most of it new and experimental. They have something which is really a glorified form of Reggie Upton's Box. I shall never laugh at the poor Bruiser again. There is a great deal in it. More in fact than he imagines. Angel's Box is able to speak and to hear. In fact I spend most of my days and nights carrying on conversations with people I never see. They are trying to psycho-analyse me. I know this sounds absurd. The Germans at the end of the war were developing this Box for the examination of prisoners. The Russians have perfected it. They don't need any of the old physical means of persuasion. They can see into the minds of the most obdurate. The Existentialists in Paris first started using it for psycho-analysing people who would not voluntarily submit to treatment. They first break the patient's nerve by acting all sorts of violent scenes which he thinks are really happening. They confuse him until he doesn't distinguish between natural sounds and those they induce. They make all kinds of preposterous accusations against him. Then when they get him in a receptive mood they start on their psycho-analysis. As you can imagine it's a hellish invention in the wrong hands. Angel's are very much the wrong hands. He's an amateur and a conceited ass. That young man who came to the hotel with my tickets was there to measure my 'life-waves'. I should have thought they could equally well have got them on board. Perhaps there is some particular gadget they have to get in London for each person. I don't know. There is still a good deal about the whole business I don't know. When I get back I will make inquiries. I'm not the first person they've tried it on. They drove an actor to suicide. I rather suspect they've been at work on poor Roger Stillingfleet. In fact I think we shall find a number of our friends who have behaved oddly lately have suffered from Angel.

Anyway thay have had no success with me. I've seen through them. All they have done is to stop my working. So I am leaving them. I shall go straight to the Galleface in Colombo and look round from there for a quiet place in the hills. I'll telegraph when I arrive which should be about the time you get this letter.

All love

G.

'Gilbert,' said Angel, 'you can't send that letter.'

'I am certainly going to – by air mail from Port Said.'

'It's going to make trouble.'

'I hope so.'

'You don't understand the importatce of the work we're doing. Did you see the *Cocktail Party*? Do you remember the second act? We are like the people in that, a little band doing good, sworn to secrecy, working behind the scenes every-where – '

'You're a pretentious busy-body.'

'Look here, Gilbert – '

'And who the devil said you might use my Christian name?'

'Gilbert.'

'Mr Pinfold to you.'

'Mr Pinfold, I admit we've not handled your case properly. We'll leave you in peace if you'll destroy that letter.'

'*I* am leaving *you*, my good Angel. The question does not arise.'

Goneril cut in: 'We'll give you hell for this, Gilbert. We'll get you and you know it. We'll never let you go. We've got you.'

'Oh, shut up,' said Mr Pinfold.

He felt himself master of the field: caught unawares, with unfamiliar barbarous weapons, treacherously ambushed when, as it were, he was under the cover of the Red Cross, he had rallied and routed the enemy. Their grand strategy had been utterly frustrated. All they could do now was snipe.

This they did continuously during the last twenty-four hours of the voyage. Mr Pinfold went about his business in a babble of jeering, threatening, cajoling voices. He gave notice to the purser of his intention of leaving the ship and sent a message by wireless engaging an air passage to Colombo.

'You can't go, Gilbert. They won't let you off the ship. The doctor has you under observation. He'll keep you in a home because you're mad, Gilbert . . . You haven't the money. You can't hire a car . . . Your passport expired last week . . . They won't take traveller's cheques in Egypt . . . ' 'He's got dollars the beast.' 'Well, that's criminal. He ought to have declared them. They'll get him for that.' 'They won't let you through the military zone, Gilbert' (this was in 1954). 'The army will turn you back. Egyptian terrorists are bombing private cars on the canal road.'

Mr Pinfold fought back with the enemy's weapons. He was obliged to hear all they said. They were obliged to hear him. They could not measure his emotions, but every thought which took verbal shape in his mind was audible in Angel's headquarters and they were unable, it seemed, to disconnect their box. Mr Pinfold set out to wear them down with sheer boredom. He took a copy of *Westward Ho!* from the ship's library and read it very slowly hour by hour. At first Goneril attempted to correct his pronunciation. At first Angel pretended to find psychological significance in the varying emphasis he gave to different words. But after an hour or so they gave up these pretences and cried in frank despair: 'Gilbert, for God's sake stop.'

Then Mr Pinfold tormented them in his turn by making gibberish of the text, reading alternate lines, alternate words, reading backwards, until they pleaded for a respite. Hour after hour Mr Pinfold remorselessly read on.

On his last evening he felt magnanimous towards all except Angel and Goneril. Word had got round the passengers that he was leaving them and as he sauntered among them he noted genuine regret in the scraps of talk he overheard.

'Is it really because of that game of Mr Angel's?' he heard Mrs Benson ask.

'He's very much annoyed with all of us.'

'You can hardly blame him. I'm sorry now I took any part in it.'

'It wasn't really very funny. I never saw the point really.'

'What's more we've cost him a lot of money. He may be able to afford it, but it's unfair, all the same.'

'I never believed half they said about him.'

'I wish I'd got to know him. I believe he's really very nice.'

'He's a very distinguished man and we've behaved like a lot of badly brought up children.'

There was no hatred or ridicule now in any of their conversations. That evening before dinner, he joined the Scarfields.

'In a couple of days it will be getting hot,' she said.

'I shan't be here.'

'Not here? I thought you were going to Colombo?'

He explained the change of plan.

'Oh, what a pity,' she said with an unmistakable innocence. 'It's only after Port Said that one ever really gets to know people.'

'I think I'll dine at your table tonight.'

'Do. We've missed you.'

So Mr Pinfold returned to the Captain's table and ordered champagne for them all. None except the Captain's table knew of his imminent departure. Throughout all the tumult of the journey this little group had remained isolated and unaware of what was afoot. Mr Pinfold was still not sure of the Captain. That quiet sea-dog had turned a Nelson eye on proceedings far beyond the scope of his imagination.

'I'm sorry we shan't have you with us, particularly now you are feeling so much better,' he said, raising his glass. 'I hope you have a comfortable flight.'

'Urgent business, I suppose?' said Glover.

'Just impatience,' said Mr Pinfold.

He remained with the group. Glover gave him advice about tailors in Colombo and cool hotels in the hills suitable for literary work. When they broke up, Mr Pinfold said good-bye, for the *Caliban* was due in harbour early and all would be busy next morning.

On his way to his cabin he met the dark figure of Mr Murdoch, who stopped and spoke to him. His manner was genial and his voice richly redolent of the industrial North.

'Purser tells me you're landing tomorrow,' he said. 'So am I. How do you reckon to get to Cairo?'

'I haven't really thought. Train, I suppose.'

'Ever been in a Wog train? Filthy dirty and slow. I tell you what, my firm's sending a car for me. I'd be glad of your company.'

So it was arranged they should travel together.

The night still belonged to Angel and Goneril. 'Don't trust Murdoch,' they whispered. 'Murdoch is your enemy.' There was no peace in the cabin and Mr Pinfold remained on deck watching for the poor little pharos of Port Said, recognized its beam, saw the pilot come aboard with a launchful of officials in tarbooshes, saw the waterfront come clear in view, populous even at that hour with touts and scarab-sellers.

In the hubbub of early morning and the successive inter-

views with port officials Mr Pinfold was intermittently aware
that Goneril and Angel were still jabbering, still impotently
trying to obstruct. Only when at last he went down the gangway did they fall silent. Mr Pinfold had been to Port Said
often before. He had never expected to feel affection for the
place. That day he did. He watched patiently while unshaven,
smoking officials examined him, his passport, and his baggage.
He cheerfully paid a number of absurd impositions. An
English agent of Mr Murdoch's company warned them:

'. . . Pretty tricky drive at the moment. Only last week
there was a chap hired a car to go to Cairo. The Wog drove
off the road just after Ismailia into a village. He was set on, all
his luggage pinched. They even took his clothes. Not a stitch
on when the police picked him up. And all they said was
he ought to consider himself lucky they hadn't cut his
throat.'

Mr Pinfold did not care. He posted his letter to his wife.
He and Murdoch drank a bottle of beer at a café and suffered
their boots to be cleaned two or three times. The funnels of
the *Caliban* were plainly to be seen from where he sat, but no
voices came from her. Then he and Murdoch drove away out
of sight of the unhappy ship.

The road to Cairo was more warlike than he had known
it ten years back when Rommel was at the gates. They passed
through lanes of barbed wire, halted and showed passports
at numerous barriers, crept in dust behind convoys of army
trucks, each with a sentry crouched on the tailboard with a
tommy-gun at the ready. There came a longer halt and closer
scrutiny at the turning out of the Canal Zone, where swarthy,
sullen English soldiers gave place to swarthy, sullen Egyptians
in almost identical uniforms. Murdoch was a man of few
words and Mr Pinfold sat enveloped in his own impervious
peace.

Once during the war he had gone on a parachute course which had ended ignominiously with his breaking a leg in his first drop, but he treasured as the most serene and exalted experience of his life the moment of liberation when he regained consciousness after the shock of the slipstream. A quarter of a minute before he had crouched over the open man-hole in the floor of the machine, in dusk and deafening noise, trussed in harness, crowded by apprehensive fellow-tyros. Then the dispatching officer had signalled; down he had plunged into a moment of night, to come to himself in a silent, sunlit heaven, gently supported by what had seemed irksome bonds, absolutely isolated. There were other parachutes all round him holding other swaying bodies; there was an instructor on the ground bawling advice through a loud-speaker; but Mr Pinfold felt himself free of all human com-munication, the sole inhabitant of a private, delicious universe. The rapture was brief. Almost at once he knew he was not floating but falling; the field leaped up at him; a few seconds later he was lying on grass, entangled in cords, being shouted at, breathless, bruised, with a sharp pain in the shin. But in that moment of solitude prosaic, earthbound Mr Pinfold had been one with hashish-eaters and Corybantes and Californian gurus, high on the back-stairs of mysticism. His mood on the road to Cairo was barely less ecstatic.

Cairo was still pocked and gutted by the recent riots. It was thronged with stamp-dealers who had come for the sale of the royal collection. Mr Pinfold had difficulty in finding a room. Murdoch obtained one for him. There was difficulty with his air passage and there too Murdoch helped. Finally on the second day when Mr Pinfold was provided by the concierge of his hotel with all the requisite documents – including a medical certificate and a sworn statement, necessary for a halt in Arabia, that he was a Christian – and his departure was fixed for midnight, Murdoch invited him to dine with his business associates in Ghezira.

'They'll be delighted. They don't see many people from home these days. And to tell you the truth I'm glad to have a companion myself. I don't much like driving about alone after dark.'

So they went to dinner in a block of expensive modern flats. The lift was out of order. As they climbed the stairs they passed an Egyptian soldier squatting in a flat doorway, chewing nuts, with his rifle propped behind him.

'One of the old princesses,' said Murdoch, 'under house-arrest.'

Host and hostess greeted them kindly. Mr Pinfold looked about him. The drawing-room was furnished with the trophies of long residence in the East. On the chimney-piece was the framed photograph of a peer in coronation-robes. Mr Pinfold studied it.

'Surely that's Simon Dumbleton?'

'Yes, he's a great friend of ours. Do you know him?'

Before he could answer another voice broke in on that cosy scene.

'No, you don't, Gilbert,' said Goneril. 'Liar. Snob. You only pretend to know him because he's a lord.'

8

PINFOLD REGAINED

MR PINFOLD landed at Colombo three days later. He had spent one almost sleepless night in the aeroplane where a pallid Parsee sprawled and grunted and heaved beside him; and a second equally wakeful alone in a huge, teetotal hotel in Bombay. Night and day Angel, Goneril, and Margaret chattered to him in their several idioms. He was becoming like the mother of fractious children who has learned to go about her business with a mind closed to their utterances; except that he had no business. He could only sit hour after hour waiting in one place or another for meals he did not want. Sometimes from sheer boredom he spoke to Margaret and learned from her further details of the conspiracy.

'Are you still in the ship?'

'No. We got off at Aden.'

'All of you?'

'All three.'

'But the others?'

'There never were any others, Gilbert. Just my brother and sister-in-law and me. You saw our names in the passenger list, Mr and Mrs and Miss Angel. I thought you understood all that.'

'But your mother and father?'

'They're in England, at home – quite near Lychpole.'

'Never in the ship?'

'Darling, you are slow in the uptake. What you heard was

my brother. He's really awfully good at imitations. That's how he first got taken on by the B.B.C.'

'And Goneril is married to your brother? There was never anything between her and the Captain?'

'No, of course not. She's beastly but not like that. All *that* was part of the Plan.'

'I think I'm beginning to understand. You must see it's all rather confusing.' Mr Pinfold puzzled his weary head over the matter; then gave it up and asked: 'What are you doing in Aden?'

'Me? Nothing. The others have their work. It's awfully dull for me. May I talk to you sometimes? I know I'm not a bit clever but I'll try not to be a bore. I do so want company.'

'Why don't you go and see the mermaid?'

'I don't understand.'

'There used to be a mermaid at Aden in a box in one of the hotels – stuffed.'

'Don't tease, Gilbert.'

'I'm not teasing. And anyway that comes pretty badly from a member of your family. *Tease* indeed.'

'Oh, Gilbert, you don't understand. We were only trying to help you.'

'Who the devil said I needed help?'

'Don't be cross, Gilbert; not with me anyway. And you did need help you know. Often their plans work beautifully.'

'Well, you must realize by now that it hasn't worked with me.'

'Oh, no,' said Margaret sadly. 'It hasn't worked at all.'

'Then why not leave me alone?'

'They never will now, because they hate you. And I never will, never. You see I love you so. Try not to hate me, darling.'

From Cairo to Colombo he talked intermittently to Margaret. To the Angels, husband and wife, he made no answer.

Ceylon was a new country to Mr Pinfold but he had no sense of exhilaration on arrival. He was tired and sweaty. He was wearing the wrong clothes. His first act after leaving his luggage at the hotel was to seek the tailor Glover had recommended. The man promised to work all night and have three suits ready for him to try on next morning.

'You're too fat. You'll look ridiculous in them. They won't fit . . . You can't afford them . . . The tailor's lying. He won't make clothes for you,' Goneril monotonously interpolated.

Mr Pinfold returned to his hotel and wrote to his wife: '*I have arrived safe and well. There does not seem to be much to see or do in Colombo. I will move as soon as I have some clothes. I rather doubt whether I shall get any work done. I had a disappointment leaving the ship. I thought I should get out of range of those psycho-analysts and their infernal Box. But not at all. They still annoy me with the whole length of India between us. As I write this letter they keep interrupting. It will be quite impossible to do any of my book. There must be some way of cutting the "vital waves". I think it might be worth consulting Father Westmacott when I get back. He knows all about existentialism and psychology and ghosts and diabolic possession. Sometimes I wonder whether it is not literally the Devil who is molesting me.*'

He posted this by air mail. Then he sat on the terrace watching the new cheap cars drive up and away. Here, unlike Bombay, one could drink. He drank bottled English beer. The sky darkened. A thunderstorm broke. He moved from the terrace into the lofty hall. To a man at Mr Pinfold's time of life few throngs comprise only strangers. In the busy hall he was greeted by an acquaintance from New York, a collector for one of the art galleries, on his way to visit a ruined city on the other side of the island. He asked Mr Pinfold to join him.

At that moment a gentle servant appeared at his side: 'Mr Peenfold, sir, cable.'

It came from his wife and read: '*Implore you return immediately.*'

It was not like Mrs Pinfold to issue a summons of this kind. Could she be ill? Or one of the children? Had the house burned down? She would surely have given some explanation? It occurred to Mr Pinfold that she must be concerned on his account. That letter he had sent from Port Said, had it said anything to cause alarm? He answered: '*All well. Returning soon. Have written today. Off to the ruins,*' and rejoined his new companion. They dined together cheerfully, having many tastes and friends and memories in common. All that evening, though there was an undertone in his ears, Mr Pinfold was oblivious of the Angels. Not till late, when he was alone in his room, did the voices break through. 'We heard you, Gilbert. You were lying to that American. You've never stayed at Rhinebeck. You've never heard of Magnasco. You don't know Osbert Sitwell.'

'Oh God,' said Mr Pinfold, 'how you bore me!'

It was cooler among the ruins. There was refreshment in the leafy roads, in the spectacle of grey elephants and orange-robed, shaven-pated monks ambling meditatively in the dust. They stopped at rest-houses where they were greeted and zealously served by old servants of the British Raj. Mr Pinfold enjoyed himself. On the way back they stopped at the shrine of Kandy and saw the Buddha's tooth ceremoniously exposed. This seemed to exhaust the artistic resources of the island. The American was on his way farther east. They parted company four days later at the hotel in Colombo where they had met. Mr Pinfold was alone once more and at a loose end. He found waiting for him a pile of clothes from the tailor and another cable from his wife: '*Both your letters received. Am coming to join you.*'

It had been handed in at Lychpole that morning.

'He hates his wife,' said Goneril. 'She bores you, doesn't she, Gilbert? You don't want to go home, do you? You dread seeing her again.'

That decided him. He cabled: *'Returning at once'* and set about his preparations.

The three suits were pale pinkish buff ('How smart you look,' cried Margaret); they were not entirely useless. He wore them on successive days; first in Colombo.

It was Sunday and he went to Mass for the first time since he had been struck ill. The voices followed him. The taxi took him first to the Anglican church. '. . . What's the difference, Gilbert? It's all nonsense anyway. You don't believe in God. There's no one here to show off to. No one will listen to your prayers – except us. *We* shall hear them. You're going to pray to be left alone, aren't you, Gilbert? Aren't you? But only we will hear and we won't let you alone. Never, Gilbert, never . . .' But when he reached the little Catholic church, which ironically enough, he found to be dedicated to St Michael and the Angels, only Margaret followed him into the dusky, crowded interior. She knew the Mass and made the Latin responses in clear, gentle tones. Epistle and Gospel were read in the vernacular. There was a short sermon, during which Mr Pinfold asked: 'Margaret, are you a Catholic?'

'In a way.'

'In what way?'

'That's something you mustn't ask.'

Then she rose with him to recite the creed and later, at the sacring-bell, she urged: 'Pray for *them*, Gilbert. They need prayers.' But Mr Pinfold could not pray for Angel and Goneril.

On Monday he arranged his passage. On Tuesday he spent another ineffably tedious night at Bombay. On Wednesday

night at Karachi he changed back into winter clothes. Somewhere on the sea they may have passed the *Caliban*. They steered
far clear of Aden. Across the Moslem world the voices of hate
pursued Mr Pinfold. It was when they reached Christendom
that Angel changed his tune. At breakfast at Rome Mr Pinfold
addressed the waiter, who spoke rather good English, in
rather bad Italian. It was an affectation which Goneril was
quick to exploit.

'No spikka da Eenglish,' she jeered. 'Kissa da monk. Dolce
far niente.'

'Shut up,' said Angel sharply. 'We've had enough of that.
I've got to talk to Gilbert seriously. Listen, Gilbert, I've got a
proposition to make.'

But Mr Pinfold would not answer.

Intermittently throughout the flight to Paris Angel attempted to open a discussion.

'Gilbert, do listen to me. We've got to come to some
arrangement. Time's getting short. Gilbert, old boy, do be
reasonable.'

His tone changed from friendliness to cajolery, at length to
a whine; the voice which had been so well-bred was now the
underdog's voice which Mr Pinfold remembered from their
brief meeting at Lychpole.

'Do speak to him, Gilbert,' Margaret pleaded. 'He's really
very worried.'

'So he should be. If your miserable brother wants me to
reply he can address me properly, as "Mr Pinfold", or "Sir".'

'Very well, Mr Pinfold, sir,' said Angel.

'That's better. Now what have you to say?'

'I want to apologize. I've made a mess of the whole Plan.'

'You certainly have.'

'It was a serious scientific experiment. Then I let personal
malice interfere. I'm sorry, Mr Pinfold.'

'Well, keep quiet then.'

'That's just what I was going to suggest. Look here, Gil—Mr Pinfold, sir – let's do a deal. I'll switch off the apparatus. I promise on my honour we'll none of us ever worry you again. All we ask in return is that you don't say anything to anyone in England about us. It could ruin our whole work if it got talked about. Just say nothing, and you'll never hear from us again. Tell your wife you had noises in the head through taking those grey pills. Tell her anything you like but tell her it's all over. She'll believe you. She'll be delighted to hear it.'

'I'll think it over,' said Mr Pinfold.

He thought it over. There were strong attractions in the bargain. Could Angel be trusted? He was in a panic now at the prospect of getting into trouble with the B.B.C. –

'Not the B.B.C., darling,' said Margaret. 'It isn't them that worry him. They know all about his experiments. It's Reggie Graves-Upton. *He* must never know. He's a sort of cousin, you see, and he would tell our aunt and father and mother and everyone. It would cause the most frightful complications. Gilbert, you must never tell *anyone*, promise, especially not cousin Reggie.'

'And you, Meg,' said Mr Pinfold in bantering but fond tones, 'are you going to leave me alone too?'

'Oh, Gilbert, dearest, it's not a thing to joke about. I've so loved being with you. I shall miss you more than anyone I've ever known in my life. I shall never forget you. If my brother switches off it will be a kind of death for me. But I know I have to suffer. I'll be brave. You *must* accept the offer, Gilbert.'

'I'll let you know before I reach London,' said Mr Pinfold.

Presently they were over England.

'Well,' said Angel, 'what's your answer?'

'I said "London".'

Later they were over London airport. 'Fasten your belts please. No smoking.'

'Here we are,' said Angel. 'Speak up. Is it a deal?'

'I don't call this London,' said Mr Pinfold.

He had cabled to his wife from Rome that he would go straight to the hotel they always used. He did not wait for the other passengers to board the bus. Instead he hired a car. Not until they were in the borough of Acton did he reply to Angel. Then he said:

'The answer is: no.'

'You can't mean it.' Angel was unaffectedly aghast. 'Why, Mr Pinfold, sir? Why?'

'First, because I don't accept your word of honour. You don't know what honour is. Secondly, I thoroughly dislike you and your revolting wife. You have been extremely offensive to me and I intend to make you suffer for it. Thirdly, I think your plans, your work as you call it, highly dangerous. You've driven one man to suicide, perhaps others too, that I don't know about. You tried to drive me. Heaven knows what you've done to Roger Stillingfleet. Heaven knows who you may attack next. Apart from any private resentment I feel, I regard you as a public menace that has got to be silenced.'

'All right, Gilbert, if that's the way you want it – '

'Don't call me "Gilbert" and don't talk like a film gangster.'

'All right, Gilbert. You'll pay for this.'

But there was no confidence to his threats. Angel was a beaten man and knew it.

'Mrs Pinfold arrived an hour ago,' the concierge told him. 'She is waiting for you in your room.'

Mr Pinfold took the lift, walked down the corridor, and

opened the door, with Goneril and Angel raucous on either side. He was shy of his wife, when they met.

'You *look* all right,' she said.

'I *am* all right. I have this trouble I wrote to you about, but I hope I can get it cleared up. I'm sorry not to be more affectionate, but it's a little embarasssing having three people listening to everything one says.'

'Yes,' said Mrs Pinfold. 'It must be. I can see that. Have you had luncheon?'

'Hours ago, in Paris. Of course there's the difference of an hour.'

'I've had none. I'll order something now.'

'How you hate her, Gilbert! How she bores you!' said Goneril.

'Don't believe a word she says,' said Angel.

'She's very pretty,' Margaret conceded, 'and very kind. But she is not good enough for you. I suppose you think I'm jealous. Well, I am.'

'I'm sorry to be so uncommunicative,' said Mr Pinfold. 'You see these abominable people keep talking to me.'

'Most distracting,' said Mrs Pinfold.

'Most.'

The waiter brought a tray. When he had gone Mrs Pinfold said: 'You know you've got it all wrong about this Mr Angel. As soon as I got your letter I telephoned to Arthur at the B.B.C. and inquired. Angel has been in England all the time.'

'*Don't listen to her. She's lying.*'

Mr Pinfold was dumbfounded.

'Are you absolutely sure?'

'Ask them yourself.'

Mr Pinfold went to the telephone. He had a friend named Arthur high in the talks department.

'Arthur that fellow who came down to interview me last

summer, Angel – haven't you sent him to Aden ... you haven't? He's in England now? ... No, I don't want to speak to him ... It's just that I ran across someone rather like him on board ship ... Good-bye ... Well,' he said to his wife, 'I simply don't know what to make of this.'

'I may as well tell you the truth,' said Angel. 'We never were in that ship. We worked the whole thing from the studio in England.'

'They must be working the whole thing from a studio in England,' said Mr Pinfold.

'My poor darling,' said Mrs Pinfold, 'no one's "worked" anything. You're imagining it all. Just to make sure I asked Father Westmacott as you suggested. He says the whole thing's utterly impossible. There just isn't any sort of invention by the Gestapo or the B.B.C. or the Existentialists or the psychoanalysts – nothing at all, the least like what you think.'

'No Box?'

'No Box.'

'Don't believe her. She's lying. She's lying,' said Goneril but with every word her voice dwindled as though a great distance was being put between them. Her last word was little more than the thin grating of a slate-pencil.

'You mean that everything I've heard said, I've been saying to myself? It's hardly conceivable.'

'It's perfectly true, darling,' said Margaret. 'I never had a brother or a sister-in-law, no father, no mother, nothing ... I don't exist, Gilbert. There isn't any me, anywhere at all ... but I do love you, Gilbert. I don't exist but I do love ... Good-bye ... Love ... ' and her voice too trailed away, sank to a whisper, a sigh, the rustle of a pillow; then was silent.

Mr Pinfold sat in the silence. There had been other occasions of seeming release which had proved illusory. This he knew was the final truth. He was alone with his wife.

'They've gone,' he said at length. 'In that minute. Gone for good.'

'I hope that's true. What are we going to do now? I couldn't make any plans till I knew what sort of state I'd find you in. Father Westmacott gave me the name of a man he says we can trust.'

'A looney doctor?'

'A psychologist – but a Catholic so he must be all right.'

'No,' said Mr Pinfold. 'I've had enough of psychology. How about taking the tea train home?'

Mrs Pinfold hesitated. She had come to London prepared to see her husband into a nursing-home. She said: 'Are you sure you oughtn't to see somebody.'

'I might see Drake,' said Mr Pinfold.

So they went to Paddington and took their seats in the restaurant car. It was full of neighbours returning from a day's shopping. They ate toasted buns and the familiar landscape rolled past invisible in the dark and misted window-panes.

'We heard you'd gone to the tropics, Gilbert.'

'Just back.'

'You didn't stay long. Was it boring?'

'No,' said Mr Pinfold, 'not the least boring. It was most exciting. But I had enough.'

Their neighbours always had thought Mr Pinfold rather odd.

'But it *was* exciting,' said Mr Pinfold when he and his wife were alone in the car driving home. 'It was the most exciting thing, really, that ever happened to me,' and during the days which followed he recounted every detail of his long ordeal.

The hard frost had given place to fog and intermittent sleet. The house was as cold as ever but Mr Pinfold was content to sit over the fire and, like a warrior returned from a hard fought victory, relive his trials, endurances and achievements. No sound troubled him from that other half-world into which he had stumbled but there was nothing dreamlike about his memories. They remained undiminished and unobscured, as sharp and hard as any event of his waking life. 'What I can't understand is this,' he said: 'If I was supplying all the information to the Angels, why did I tell them such a lot of rot? I mean to say, if I wanted to draw up an indictment of myself I could make a far blacker and more plausible case than they did. I can't understand.'

Mr Pinfold never has understood this; nor has anyone been able to suggest a satisfactory explanation.

'You know,' he said, some evenings later, 'I was very near accepting Angel's offer. Supposing I had, and the voices had stopped just as they have done now, I should have believed that that infernal Box existed. All my life I should have lived in the fear that at any moment the whole thing might start up again. Or for all I knew they might just have been listening all the time and not saying anything. It would have been an awful situation.'

'It was very brave of you to turn down the offer,' said Mrs Pinfold.

'It was sheer bad temper,' said Mr Pinfold quite truthfully.

'All the same, I think you ought to see a doctor. There must have been something the matter with you.'

'Just those pills,' said Mr Pinfold.

They were his last illusion. When finally Dr Drake came Mr Pinfold said: 'Those grey pills you gave me. They were pretty strong.'

'They seem to have worked,' said Dr Drake.

'Could they have made me hear voices?'

'Good heavens, no.'

'Not if they were mixed with bromide and chloral?'

'There wasn't any chloral in the mixture I gave you.'

'No. But to tell you the truth I had a bottle of my own.'

Dr Drake did not seem shocked by the revelation. 'That is always the trouble with patients,' he said. 'One never knows what else they're taking on the quiet. I've known people make themselves thoroughly ill.'

'I *was* thoroughly ill. I heard voices for nearly a fortnight.'

'And they've stopped now?'

'Yes.'

'And you've stopped the bromide and chloral?'

'Yes.'

'Then I don't think we have far to look. I should keep off that mixture if I were you. It can't be the right thing for you. I'll send something else. Those voices were pretty offensive, I suppose?'

'Abominable. How did you know?'

'They always are. Lots of people hear voices from time to time – nearly always offensive.'

'You don't think he ought to see a psychologist?' asked Mrs Pinfold.

'He can if he likes, of course, but it sounds like a perfectly simple case of poisoning to me.'

'That's a relief,' said Mrs Pinfold, but Mr Pinfold accepted this diagnosis less eagerly. He knew, and the others did not know – not even his wife, least of all his medical adviser – that he had endured a great ordeal, and unaided, had emerged the victor. There was a triumph to be celebrated, even if a mocking slave stood always beside him in his chariot reminding him of mortality.

Next day was Sunday. After Mass Mr Pinfold said:

'You know I can't face the Bruiser. It's going to be several weeks before I can talk to him about his Box. Have a fire lighted in the library. I'm going to do some writing.'

As the wood crackled and a barely perceptible warmth began to spread among the chilly shelves, Mr Pinfold sat down to work for the first time since his fiftieth birthday. He took the pile of manuscript, his unfinished novel, from the drawer and glanced through it. The story was still clear in his mind. He knew what had to be done. But there was more urgent business first, a hamper to be unpacked of fresh, rich experience – perishable goods.

He returned the manuscript to the drawer, spread a new quire of foolscap before him, and wrote in his neat, steady hand:

The Ordeal of Gilbert Pinfold
A Conversation Piece
Chapter One
Portrait of the Artist in Middle-age

Tactical Exercise

*

JOHN VERNEY married Elizabeth in 1938, but it was not until the winter of 1945 that he came to hate her steadily and fiercely. There had been countless brief gusts of hate before this, for it was a thing which came easily to him. He was not what is normally described as a bad-tempered man, rather the reverse; a look of fatigue and abstraction was the only visible sign of the passion which possessed him, as others are possessed by laughter or desire, several times a day.

During the war he passed among those he served with as a phlegmatic fellow. He did not have his good or his bad days; they were all uniformly good or bad; good in that he did what had to be done, expeditiously without ever 'getting in a flap' or 'going off the deep end'; bad from the intermittent, invisible sheet-lightning of hate which flashed and flickered deep inside him at every obstruction or reverse. In his orderly room when, as a company commander, he faced the morning procession of defaulters and malingerers; in the mess when the subalterns disturbed his reading by playing the wireless; at the Staff College when the 'syndicate' disagreed with his solution; at Brigade H.Q. when the staff-sergeant mislaid a file or the telephone orderly muddled a call; when the driver of his car missed a turning; later, in hospital, when the doctor seemed to look cursorily at his wound and the nurses stood gossiping jauntily at the beds of more likeable patients instead of doing their duty to him – in all the annoyances of army life which others dismissed with an oath and a shrug, John

Verney's eyelids drooped wearily, a tiny grenade of hate exploded, and the fragments rang and ricocheted round the steel walls of his mind.

There had been less to annoy him before the war. He had some money and the hope of a career in politics. Before marriage he served his apprenticeship to the Liberal party in two hopeless by-elections. The Central Office then rewarded him with a constituency in outer London which offered a fair chance in the next general election. In the eighteen months before the war he nursed this constituency from his flat in Belgravia and travelled frequently on the Continent to study political conditions. These studies convinced him that war was inevitable; he denounced the Munich agreement pungently and secured a commission in the Territorial Army.

Into the peacetime life Elizabeth fitted unobtrusively. She was his cousin. In 1938 she had reached the age of twenty-six, four years his junior, without falling in love. She was a calm, handsome young woman, an only child, with some money of her own and more to come. As a girl, in her first season, an injudicious remark, let slip and overheard, got her the reputation of cleverness. Those who knew her best ruthlessly called her 'deep'.

Thus condemned to social failure, she languished in the ballrooms of Pont Street for another year and then settled down to a life of concert-going and shopping with her mother, until she surprised her small circle of friends by marrying John Verney. Courtship and consummation were tepid, cousinly, harmonious. They agreed, in face of coming war, to remain childless. No one knew what Elizabeth felt or thought about anything. Her judgements were mainly negative, deep or dull as you cared to take them. She had none of the appearance of a woman likely to inflame great hate.

John Verney was discharged from the Army early in 1945 with a M.C. and one leg, for the future, two inches shorter than the other. He found Elizabeth living in Hampstead with her parents, his uncle and aunt. She had kept him informed of the changes in her condition, but, preoccupied, he had not clearly imagined them. Their flat had been requisitioned by a government office; their furniture and books sent to a repository and totally lost, partly burned by a bomb, partly pillaged by firemen. Elizabeth, who was a linguist, had gone to work in a clandestine branch of the Foreign Office.

Her parents' house had once been a substantial Georgian villa overlooking the Heath. John Verney arrived there early in the morning after a crowded night's journey from Liverpool. The wrought-iron railings and gates had been rudely torn away by the salvage collectors, and in the front garden, once so neat, weeds and shrubs grew in a rank jungle trampled at night by courting soldiers. The back garden was a single, small bomb-crater; heaped clay, statuary, and the bricks and glass of ruined greenhouses; dry stalks of willow-herb stood breast high over the mounds. All the windows were gone from the back of the house, replaced by shutters of card and board, which put the main rooms in perpetual darkness. 'Welcome to Chaos and Old Night,' said his uncle genially.

There were no servants; the old had fled, the young had been conscripted for service. Elizabeth made him some tea before leaving for her office.

Here he lived, lucky, Elizabeth told him, to have a home. Furniture was unprocurable, furnished flats commanded a price beyond their income, which was now taxed to a bare wage. They might have found something in the country, but Elizabeth, being childless, could not get release from her work. Moreover, he had his constituency.

This, too, was transformed. A factory wired round like a

prisoner-of-war camp stood in the public gardens. The streets surrounding it, once the trim houses of potential Liberals, had been bombed, patched, confiscated, and filled with an immigrant proletarian population. Every day he received a heap of complaining letters from constituents exiled in provincial boarding-houses. He had hoped that his decoration and his limp might earn him sympathy, but he found the new inhabitants indifferent to the fortunes of war. Instead they showed a sceptical curiosity about Social Security. 'They're nothing but a lot of reds,' said the Liberal agent.

'You mean I shan't get in?'

'Well, we'll give them a good fight. The Tories are putting up a Battle-of-Britain pilot. I'm afraid he'll get most of what's left of the middle-class vote.'

In the event John Verney came bottom of the poll, badly. A rancorous Jewish schoolteacher was elected. The Central Office paid his deposit, but the election had cost him dear. And when it was over there was absolutely nothing for John Verney to do.

He remained in Hampstead, helped his aunt make the beds after Elizabeth had gone to her office, limped to the green-grocer and fishmonger, and stood, full of hate, in the queues; helped Elizabeth wash up at night. They ate in the kitchen, where his aunt cooked deliciously the scanty rations. His uncle went three days a week to help pack parcels for Java.

Elizabeth, the deep one, never spoke of her work, which, in fact, was concerned with setting up hostile and oppressive governments in Eastern Europe. One evening at a restaurant, a man came and spoke to her, a tall young man whose sallow aquiline face was full of intellect and humour. 'That's the head of my department,' she said. 'He's so amusing.'

'Looks like a Jew.'

'I believe he is. He's a strong Conservative and hates the

work,' she added hastily, for since his defeat in the election John had become fiercely anti-Semitic.

'There is absolutely no need to work for the State now,' he said. 'The war's over.'

'Our work is just beginning. They won't let any of us go. You must understand what conditions are in this country.'

It often fell to Elizabeth to explain 'conditions' to him. Strand by strand, knot by knot, through the coalless winter, she exposed the vast net of governmental control which had been woven in his absence. He had been reared in traditional Liberalism and the system revolted him. More than this, it had him caught, personally, tripped up, tied, tangled; wherever he wanted to go, whatever he wanted to do or have done, he found himself baffled and frustrated. And as Elizabeth explained she found herself defending. This regulation was necessary to avoid that ill; such a country was suffering, as Britain was not, for having neglected such a precaution; and so on, calmly and reasonably.

'I know it's maddening, John, but you must realize it's the same for everyone.'

'That's what all you bureaucrats want,' he said. 'Equality through slavery. The two-class state – proletarians and officials.'

Elizabeth was part and parcel of it. She worked for the State and the Jews. She was a collaborator with the new, alien, occupying power. And as the winter wore on and the gas burned feebly in the stove, and the rain blew in through the patched windows, as at length spring came and buds broke in the obscene wilderness round the house, Elizabeth in his mind became something more important. She became a symbol. For just as soldiers in far-distant camps think of their wives, with a tenderness they seldom felt at home, as the embodiment of all the good things they have left behind, wives who perhaps were scolds and drabs, but in the desert and jungle become transfigured until their trite air-letters become texts of hope, so Elizabeth grew in John Verney's despairing mind to more than human malevolence as the archpriestess and maenad of the century of the common man.

'You aren't looking well, John,' said his aunt. 'You and Elizabeth ought to get away for a bit. She is due for leave at Easter.'

'The State is granting her a supplementary ration of her husband's company, you mean. Are we sure she has filled in all the correct forms? Or are commissars of her rank above such things?'

Uncle and aunt laughed uneasily. John made his little jokes with such an air of weariness, with such a droop of the eyelids that they sometimes struck chill in that family circle. Elizabeth regarded him gravely and silently.

John was far from well. His leg was in constant pain so that he no longer stood in queues. He slept badly; as also, for the first time in her life, did Elizabeth. They shared a room now, for the winter rains had brought down ceilings in many parts of the shaken house and the upper rooms were thought to be unsafe. They had twin beds on the ground floor in what had once been her father's library.

In the first days of his homecoming John had been amorous. Now he never approached her. They lay night after night six feet apart in the darkness. Once when John had been awake for two hours he turned on the lamp that stood on the table between them. Elizabeth was lying with her eyes wide open staring at the ceiling.

'I'm sorry. Did I wake you?'

'I haven't been asleep.'

'I thought I'd read for a bit. Will it disturb you?'

'Not at all.'

She turned away. John read for an hour. He did not know whether she was awake or asleep when he turned off the light.

Often after that he longed to put on the light, but was afraid to find her awake and staring. Instead, he lay, as others lie in a luxurious rapture of love, hating her.

It did not occur to him to leave her; or, rather, it did occur from time to time, but he hopelessly dismissed the thought. Her life was bound tight to his; her family was his family; their finances were intertangled and their expectations lay together in the same quarters. To leave her would be to start fresh, alone and naked in a strange world; and lame and weary at the age of thirty-eight, John Verney had not the heart to move.

He loved no one else. He had nowhere to go, nothing to do. Moreover he suspected, of late, that it would not hurt her if he went. And, above all, the single steadfast desire left to him was to do her ill. 'I wish she were dead,' he said to himself as he lay awake at night. 'I wish she were dead.'

Sometimes they went out together. As the winter passed, John took to dining once or twice a week at his club. He assumed that on these occasions she stayed at home, but one morning it transpired that she too had dined out the evening before. He did not ask with whom, but his aunt did, and Elizabeth replied, 'Just someone from the office.'

'The Jew?' John asked.

'As a matter of fact, it was.'

'I hope you enjoyed it.'

'Quite. A beastly dinner, of course, but he's very amusing.'

One night when he returned from his club, after a dismal little dinner and two crowded Tube journeys, he found Elizabeth in bed and deeply asleep. She did not stir when he entered. Unlike her normal habit, she was snoring. He stood for a minute, fascinated by this new and unlovely aspect of her,

her head thrown back, her mouth open and slightly dribbling at the corner. Then he shook her. She muttered something, turned over, and slept heavily and soundlessly.

Half an hour later, as he was striving to compose himself for sleep, she began to snore again. He turned on the light, and looked at her more closely and noticed with surprise, which suddenly changed to joyous hope, that there was a tube of unfamiliar pills, half empty, beside her on the bed table.

He examined it. '24 *Comprimés narcotiques, hypnotiques*,' he read, and then in large scarlet letters, 'NE PAS DÉPASSER DEUX.' He counted those which were left. Eleven.

With tremulous butterfly wings hope began to flutter in his heart, became a certainty. He felt a fire kindle and spread inside him until he was deliciously suffused in every limb and organ. He lay, listening to the snores, with the pure excitement of a child on Christmas Eve. 'I shall wake up tomorrow and find her dead,' he told himself, as once he had felt the flaccid stocking at the foot of his bed and told himself, 'Tomorrow I shall wake up and find it full.' Like a child, he longed to sleep to hasten the morning and, like a child, he was wildly ecstatically sleepless. Presently he swallowed two of the pills himself and almost at once was unconscious.

Elizabeth always rose first to make breakfast for the family. She was at the dressing-table when sharply, without drowsiness, his memory stereoscopically clear about the incidents of the night before, John awoke. 'You've been snoring,' she said.

Disappointment was so intense that at first he could not speak. Then he said, 'You snored, too, last night.'

'It must be the sleeping-tablet I took. I must say it gave me a good night.'

'Only one?'

'Yes, two's the most that's safe.'

'Where did you get them?'

'A friend at the office – the one you called the Jew. He has them prescribed by a doctor for when he's working too hard. I told him I wasn't sleeping, so he gave me half a bottle.'

'Could he get me some?'

'I expect so. He can do most things like that.'

So he and Elizabeth began to drug themselves regularly and passed long, vacuous nights. But often John delayed, letting the beatific pill lie beside his glass of water, while knowing the vigil was terminable at will, he postponed the joy of unconsciousness, heard Elizabeth's snores, and hated her sumptuously.

One evening while the plans for the holiday were still under discussion, John and Elizabeth went to the cinema. The film was a murder story of no great ingenuity but with showy scenery. A bride murdered her husband by throwing him out of a window, down a cliff. Things were made easy for her by his taking a lonely lighthouse for their honeymoon. He was very rich and she wanted his money. All she had to do was to confide in the local doctor and a few neighbours that her husband frightened her by walking in his sleep; she doped his coffee, dragged him from the bed to the balcony – a feat of some strength – where she had already broken away a yard of balustrade, and rolled him over. Then she went back to bed, gave the alarm the next morning, and wept over the mangled body which was presently discovered half awash on the rocks. Retribution overtook her later, but at the time the thing was a complete success.

'I wish it were as easy as that,' thought John, and in a few hours the whole tale had floated away in those lightless attics of the mind where films and dreams and funny stories lie spider-shrouded for a lifetime unless, as sometimes happens, an intruder brings them to light.

Such a thing happened a few weeks later when John and Elizabeth went for their holiday. Elizabeth found the place.

It belonged to someone in her office. It was named Good Hope Fort, and stood on the Cornish coast. 'It's only just been derequisitioned,' she said; 'I expect we shall find it in pretty bad condition.'

'We're used to that,' said John. It did not occur to him that she should spend her leave anywhere but with him. She was as much part of him as his maimed and aching leg.

They arrived on a gusty April afternoon after a train journey of normal discomfort. A taxi drove them eight miles from the station, through deep Cornish lanes, past granite cottages and disused, archaic tin-workings. They reached the village which gave the houses its postal address, passed through it and out along a track which suddenly emerged from its high banks into open grazing land on the cliff's edge, high, swift clouds and sea-birds wheeling overhead, the turf at their feet alive with fluttering wild flowers, salt in the air, below them the roar of the Atlantic breaking on the rocks, a middle-distance of indigo and white tumbled waters and beyond it the serene arc of the horizon. Here was the house.

'Your father,' said John, 'would now say, "Your castle hath a pleasant seat".'

'Well, it has rather, hasn't it?'

It was a small stone building on the very edge of the cliff, built a century or so ago for defensive purposes, converted to a private house in the years of peace, taken again by the Navy during the war as a signal station, now once more reverting to gentler uses. Some coils of rusty wire, a mast, the concrete foundations of a hut, gave evidence of its former masters.

They carried their things into the house and paid the taxi.

'A woman comes up every morning from the village. I said we shouldn't want her this evening. I see she's left us some oil for the lamps. She's got a fire going too, bless her, and plenty of wood. Oh, and look what I've got as a present from father. I promised not to tell you until we arrived. A bottle of whisky. Wasn't it sweet of him. He's been hoarding his ration for three months. . . . ' Elizabeth talked brightly as she began to arrange the luggage. 'There's a room for each of us. This is the only proper living-room, but there's a study in case you feel like doing any work. I believe we shall be quite comfortable. . . . '

The living-room was built with two stout bays, each with a French window opening on a balcony which over-hung the sea. John opened one and the sea-wind filled the room. He stepped out, breathed deeply, and then said suddenly: 'Hullo, this is dangerous.'

At one place, between the windows, the cast-iron balustrade had broken away and the stone ledge lay open over the cliff. He looked at the gap and at the foaming rocks below, momentarily puzzled. The irregular polyhedron of memory rolled uncertainly and came to rest.

He had been here before, a few weeks ago, on the gallery of the lighthouse in that swiftly forgotten film. He stood there looking down. It was exactly thus that the waves had come swirling over the rocks, had broken and dropped back with the spray falling about them. This was the sound they had made; this was the broken ironwork and the sheer edge.

Elizabeth was still talking in the room, her voice drowned by wind and sea. John returned to the room, shut and fastened the door. In the quiet she was saying '. . . only got the furniture out of store last week. He left the woman from the village to arrange it. She's got some queer ideas, I must say. Just look where she put . . . '

'What did you say this house was called?'

'Good Hope.'

'A good name.'

That evening John drank a glass of his father-in-law's whisky, smoked a pipe, and planned. He had been a good tactician. He made a leisurely, mental 'appreciation of the situation'. Object: murder.

When they rose to go to bed he asked: 'You packed the tablets?'

'Yes, a new tube. But I am sure I shan't want any tonight.'

'Neither shall I,' said John, 'the air is wonderful.'

During the following days he considered the tactical problem. It was entirely simple. He had the 'staff-solution' already. He considered it in the words and form he had used in the Army. '. . . Courses open to the enemy . . . achievement of surprise . . . consolidation of success.' The staff-solution was exemplary. At the beginning of the first week, he began to put it into execution.

Already, by easy stages, he had made himself known in the village. Elizabeth was a friend of the owner; he the returned hero, still a little strange in civvy street. 'The first holiday my wife and I have had together for six years,' he told them in the golf club and, growing more confidential at the bar, hinted that they were thinking of making up for lost time and starting a family.

On another evening he spoke of war-strain, of how in this war the civilians had had a worse time of it than the services. His wife, for instance; stuck it all through the blitz; office work all day, bombs at night. She ought to get right away, alone somewhere for a long stretch; her nerves had suffered; nothing serious, but to tell the truth he wasn't quite happy about it. As a matter of fact he had found her walking in her sleep once or twice in London.

His companions knew of similar cases; nothing to worry about, but it wanted watching; didn't want it to develop into anything worse. Had she seen a doctor?

Not yet, John said. In fact she didn't know she had been sleep-walking. He had got her back to bed without waking her. He hoped the sea air would do her good. In fact, she seemed much better already. If she showed any more signs of the trouble when they got home, he knew a very good man to take her to.

The golf club was full of sympathy. John asked if there were a good doctor in the neighbourhood. Yes, they said, old Mackenzie in the village, a first-class man, wasted in a little place like this; not at all stick-in-the-mud. Read the latest books, psychology and all that. They couldn't think why Old Mack had never specialized and made a name for himself.

'I think I might go and talk to Old Mack about it,' said John.

'Do. You couldn't find a better fellow.'

Elizabeth had a fortnight's leave. There were still three days to go when John went off to the village to consult Dr Mackenzie. He found a grey-haired, genial bachelor in a consulting room that was more like a lawyer's office than a physician's, book-lined, dark, permeated by tobacco smoke.

Seated in the shabby leather armchair he developed in more precise language the story he had told in the golf club. Dr Mackenzie listened without comment.

'It's the first time I've run against anything like this,' he concluded.

At length Dr Mackenzie said: 'You got pretty badly knocked about in the war, Mr Verney?'

'My knee. It still gives me trouble.'

'Bad time in hospital?'

'Three months. A beastly place outside Rome.'

'There's always a good deal of nervous shock in an injury of that kind. It often persists when the wound is healed.'

'Yes, but I don't quite understand . . . '

'My dear Mr Verney, your wife asked me to say nothing about it, but I think I must tell you that she has already been here to consult me on this matter.'

'About her sleep-walking? But she can't . . . ' Then John stopped.

'My dear fellow, I quite understand. She thought you didn't know. Twice lately you've been out of bed and she had to lead you back. She knows all about it.'

John could find nothing to say.

'It's not the first time,' Dr Mackenzie continued, 'that I've been consulted by patients who have told me their symptoms and said they had come on behalf of friends or relations. Usually it's girls who think they're in a family way. It's an interesting feature of your case that you should want to ascribe the trouble to someone else, probably the decisive feature. I've given your wife the name of a man in London who I think will be able to help you. Meanwhile I can advise plenty of exercise, light meals at night . . . '

John Verney limped back to Good Hope Fort in a state of consternation. Security had been compromised; the operation must be cancelled; initiative had been lost . . . all the phrases of the tactical school came to his mind, but he was still numb after this unexpected reverse. A vast and naked horror peeped at him and was thrust aside.

When he got back Elizabeth was laying the supper table. He stood on the balcony and stared at the gaping rails with eyes smarting with disappointment. It was dead calm that evening. The rising tide lapped and fell and mounted again silently among the rocks below. He stood gazing down, then he turned back into the room.

There was one large drink left in the whisky bottle. He poured it out and swallowed it. Elizabeth brought in the supper and they sat down. Gradually his mind grew a little calmer. They usually ate in silence. At last he said: 'Elizabeth, why did you tell the doctor I had been walking in my sleep?'

She quietly put down the plate she had been holding and looked at him curiously. 'Why?' she said gently. 'Because I was worried, of course. I didn't think you knew about it.'

'But have I been?'

'Oh yes, several times – in London and here. I didn't think it mattered at first, but the night before last I found you on the balcony, quite near that dreadful hole in the rails. I was really frightened. But it's going to be all right now. Dr Mackenzie has given me the name . . . '

It was possible, thought John Verney; nothing was more likely.

He had lived night and day for ten days thinking of that opening, of the sea and rock below, the ragged ironwork and the sharp edge of stone. He suddenly felt defeated, sick and stupid, as he had as he lay on the Italian hillside with his smashed knee. Then as now he had felt weariness even more than pain.

'Coffee, darling.'

Suddenly he roused himself. 'No,' he almost shouted. 'No, no, no.'

'Darling, what is the matter? Don't get excited. Are you feeling ill? Lie down on the sofa near the window.'

He did as he was told. He felt so weary that he could barely move from his chair.

'Do you think coffee would keep you awake, love? You look quite fit to drop already. There, lie down.'

He lay down, like the tide slowly mounting among the

rocks below, sleep rose and spread in his mind. He nodded and woke with a start.

'Shall I open the window, darling, and give you some air?'

'Elizabeth,' he said, 'I feel as if I have been drugged.' Like the rocks below the window – now awash, now emerging clear from falling water; now awash again deeper; now barely visible, mere patches on the face of gentle eddying foam – his brain was softly drowning. He roused himself, as children do in nightmare, still scared, still half asleep. 'I can't be drugged,' he said loudly, 'I never touched the coffee.'

'Drugs in the coffee?' said Elizabeth gently, like a nurse soothing a fractious child. 'Drugs in the *coffee*? What an absurd idea. That's the kind of thing that only happens on the films, darling.'

He did not hear her. He was fast asleep, snoring stertorously by the open window.

Love Among the Ruins

A ROMANCE OF THE
NEAR FUTURE WITH DECORATIONS
BY VARIOUS EMINENT HANDS
INCLUDING THE
AUTHOR'S

JOHANNI MCDOUGALL
AMICO QUI NOSTRI SEDET IN
LOCO PARENTIS

I

DESPITE their promises at the last Election, the politicians had not changed the climate. The State Meteorological Institute had so far produced only an unseasonable fall of snow and two little thunderbolts no larger than apricots. The weather varied from day to day and from county to county as it had done of old, most anomalously.

This was a rich, old-fashioned Tennysonian night.

Strains of a string quartet floated out from the drawing-room windows and were lost amid the splash and murmur of the gardens. In the basin the folded lilies had left a brooding sweetness over the water. No gold fin winked in the porphyry font and any peacock which seemed to be milkily drooping in the moon-shadows was indeed a ghost, for the whole flock of them had been found mysteriously and rudely slaughtered a day or two ago in the first disturbing flush of this sudden summer.

Miles, sauntering among the sleeping flowers, was suffused with melancholy. He did not much care for music and this was his last evening at Mountjoy. Never again, perhaps, would he be free to roam these walks.

Mountjoy had been planned and planted in the years of which he knew nothing; generations of skilled and patient husbandmen had weeded and dunged and pruned; generations of dilettanti had watered it with cascades and jets; generations of collectors had lugged statuary here; all, it seemed, for his enjoyment this very night under this huge moon. Miles knew nothing of such periods and processes, but he felt an incomprehensible tidal pull towards the circum-jacent splendours.

Eleven struck from the stables. The music ceased. Miles turned back and, as he reached the terrace, the shutters began to close and the great chandeliers were one by one extin-guished. By the light of the sconces which still shone on their panels of faded satin and clouded gold, he joined the company dispersing to bed through the islands of old furniture.

His room was not one of the grand succession which lay along the garden front. Those were reserved for murderers. Nor was it on the floor above, tenanted mostly by sexual offenders. His was a humbler wing. Indeed he overlooked the luggage porch and the coal bunker. Only professional men visiting Mountjoy on professional business and very poor relations had been put here in the old days. But Miles was attached to this room, which was the first he had ever called his own in all his twenty years of Progress.

His next-door neighbour, a Mr Sweat, paused at his door to say good night. It was only now after twenty months' proximity, when Miles's time was up, that this veteran had begun to unbend. He and a man named Soapy, survivals of another age, had kept themselves to themselves, talking wistfully of cribs they had cracked, of sparklers, of snug bar-parlours where they had met their favourite fences, of strenu-ous penal days at the Scrubs and on the Moor. They had small use for the younger generation; crime, calvinism, and classical music were their interest. But at last Mr Sweat had taken to nodding, to grunting, and finally, too late for friendship, to speaking to Miles.

'What price the old strings tonight, chum?' he asked.

'I wasn't there, Mr Sweat.'

'You missed a treat. Of course nothing's ever good enough for old Soapy. Made me fair sick to hear Soapy going on all the time. The viola was scratchy, Soapy says. They played the Mozart just like it was Haydn. No feeling in the Debussy pizzicato, says Soapy.'

'Soapy knows too much.'

'Soapy knows a lot more than some I could mention, schooling or no schooling. Next time they're going to do the Grosse Fugue as the last movement of the B flat. That's something to look forward to, that is, though Soapy says no late Beethoven comes off. We'll see. Leastways, me and Soapy will; *you* won't. You're off tomorrow. Pleased?'

'Not particularly.'

'No, no more wouldn't I be. It's a funny thing but I've settled down here wonderful. Never thought I should. It all seemed a bit too posh at first. Not like the old Scrubs. But it's a real pretty place once you're used to it. Wouldn't mind settling here for a lifer if they'd let me. The trouble is there's no security in crime these days. Time was, you knew just what a job was worth, six months, three years; whatever it was, you knew where you were. Now what with prison commissioners and Preventive Custody and Corrective Treatment they can keep you in or push you out just as it suits them. It's not right.

'I'll tell you what it is, chum,' continued Mr Sweat. 'There's no understanding of crime these days like what there was. I remember when I was a nipper, the first time I came up before the beak, he spoke up straight: "My lad," he says, "you are embarking upon a course of life that can only lead to disaster and degradation in this world and everlasting damnation in the next." Now that's talking. It's plain sense and it shows a personal interest. But last time I was up, when they sent me here, they called me an "antisocial phenomenon";

said I was "maladjusted". That's no way to speak of a man
what was doing time before they was in long trousers, now
is it?'

'They said something of the same kind to me.'

'Yes and now they're giving you the push, just like you
hadn't no Rights. I tell you it's made a lot of the boys un-
comfortable your going out all of a sudden like this. Who'll
it be next time, that's what we're wondering?

'I tell you where you went wrong, chum. You didn't give
enough trouble. You made it too easy for them to say you
was cured. Soapy and me got wise to that. You remember
them birds as got done in? That was Soapy and me. They
took a lot of killing too; powerful great bastards. But we got
the evidence all hid away tidy and if there's ever any talk of
me and Soapy being "rehabilitated" we'll lay it out con-
spicuous.

'Well, so long chum. Tomorrow's my morning for
Remedial Repose so I daresay you'll be off before I get down.
Come back soon.'

'I hope so,' said Miles and turned alone into his own room.

He stood briefly at the window and gazed his last on the
cobbled yard. He made a good figure of a man, for he came
of handsome parents and all his life had been carefully fed
and doctored and exercised; well clothed too. He wore the
drab serge dress that was the normal garb of the period – only
certified homosexuals wore colours – but there were differ-
ences of fit and condition among these uniforms. Miles displayed the handiwork of tailor and valet. He belonged to a
privileged class.

The State had made him.

No clean-living, God-fearing Victorian gentleman, he; no
complete man of the renaissance; no gentil knight nor dutiful
pagan nor, even, noble savage. All that succession of past

worthies had gone its way, content to play a prelude to Miles. He was the Modern Man.

His history, as it appeared in multuplet in the filing cabinets of numberless State departments, was typical of a thousand others. Before his birth the politicians had succeeded in bringing down his father and mother to penury; they, destitute, had thrown themselves into the simple diversions of the very poor and thus, between one war and the next, set in motion a chain-reaction of divorces which scattered them and their various associates in forlorn couples all over the Free World. The aunt on whom the infant Miles had been quartered was conscribed for work in a factory and shortly afterwards died of boredom at the conveyer-belt. The child was put to safety in an Orphanage.

Huge sums were thenceforward spent upon him; sums which, fifty years earlier, would have sent whole quiversful of boys to Winchester and New College and established them in the learned professions. In halls adorned with Picassos and Légers he yawned through long periods of Constructive Play. He never lacked the requisite cubic feet of air. His diet was balanced and on the first Friday of every month he was psycho-analysed. Every detail of his adolescence was recorded and microfilmed and filed, until at the appropriate age he was transferred to the Air Force.

There were no aeroplanes at the station to which he was posted. It was an institution to train instructors to train instructors to train instructors in Personal Recreation.

There for some weeks he tended a dish-washing machine and tended it, as his adjutant testified at his trial, in an exemplary fashion. The work in itself lacked glory, but it was the normal novitiate. Men from the Orphanages provided the hard core of the Forces, a caste apart which united the formidable qualities of Janissary and Junker. Miles had been picked early

for high command. Dish-washing was only the beginning.
The adjutant, an orphan too, had himself washed both dishes
and officers' underclothes, he testified, before rising to his
present position.

Courts Martial had been abolished some years before this.
The Forces handed their defaulters over to the civil arm for
treatment. Miles came up at quarter sessions. It was plain from
the start, when Arson, Wilful Damage, Manslaughter, Pre-
judicial Conduct, and Treason were struck out of the Indictment and the whole reduced to a simple charge of Antisocial
Activity, that the sympathies of the Court were with the
prisoner.

The Station Psychologist gave his opinion that an element
of incendiarism was inseparable from adolescence. Indeed,
if checked, it might produce morbid neuroses. For his part
he thought the prisoner had performed a perfectly normal act
and, moreover, had shown more than normal intelligence in
its execution.

At this point some widows, mothers, and orphans of the
incinerated airmen set up an outcry from the public gallery
and were sharply reminded from the Bench that this was a
Court of Welfare and not a meeting of the Housewives'
Union.

The case developed into a concerted eulogy of the accused.
An attempt by the prosecution to emphasize the extent of the
damage was rebuked from the Bench.

'The Jury,' he said, 'will expunge from their memories
these sentimental details which have been most improperly
introduced.'

'May be a detail to you,' said a voice from the gallery. 'He
was a good husband to me.'

'Arrest that woman,' said the Judge.

Order was restored and the panegyrics continued.

At last the Bench summed up. He reminded the jury that it was a first principle of the New Law that no man could be held responsible for the consequences of his own acts. The jury must dismiss from their minds the consideration that much valuable property and many valuable lives had been lost and the cause of Personal Recreation gravely retarded. They had merely to decide whether in fact the prisoner had arranged inflammable material at various judiciously selected points in the Institution and had ignited them. If he had done so, and the evidence plainly indicated that he had, he contravened the Standing Orders of the Institution and was thereby liable to the appropriate penalties.

Thus directed the jury brought in a verdict of guilty coupled with a recommendation of mercy towards the various bereaved persons who from time to time in the course of the hearing had been committed for contempt. The Bench reprimanded the jury for presumption and impertinence in the matter of the prisoners held in contempt, and sentenced Miles to residence during the State's pleasure at Mountjoy Castle (the ancestral seat of a maimed v.c. of the Second World War, who had been sent to a Home for the Handicapped when the place was converted into a gaol).

The State was capricious in her pleasures. For nearly two years Miles enjoyed her particular favours. Every agreeable remedial device was applied to him and applied, it was now proclaimed, successfully. Then without warning a few days back, while he lay dozing under a mulberry tree, the unexpected blow had fallen; they had come to him, the Deputy Chief Guide and the sub-Deputy, and told him bluntly and brutally that he was rehabilitated.

Now on this last night he knew he was to wake tomorrow on a harsh world. Nevertheless he slept and was gently awoken for the last time to the familiar scent of china tea on his bed table, the thin bread and butter, the curtains drawn above the luggage porch, the sunlit kitchen-yard and the stable clock just visible behind the cut-leaf copper beech.

He breakfasted late and alone. The rest of the household were already engaged in the first community-songs of the day. Presently he was called to the Guidance Office.

Since his first day at Mountjoy, when with the other entrants Miles had been addressed at length by the Chief Guide on the Aims and Achievements of the New Penology, they had seldom met. The Chief Guide was almost always away addressing penological conferences.

The Guidance Office was the former house-keeper's room stripped now of its plush and patriotic pictures; sadly tricked out instead with standard civil-service equipment, class A.

It was full of people.

'This is Miles Plastic,' said the Chief Guide. 'Sit down, Miles. You can see from the presence of our visitors this morning what an important occasion this is.'

Miles took a chair and looked and saw seated beside the Chief Guide two elderly men whose faces were familiar from the television screen as prominent colleagues in the Coalition Government. They wore open flannel shirts, blazers with numerous pens and pencils protruding from the breast pocket, and baggy trousers. This was the dress of very high politicians.

'The Minister of Welfare and the Minister of Rest and Culture,' continued the Chief Guide. 'The stars to which we have hitched our waggon. Have the press got the handout?'

'Yes, Chief.'

'And the photographers are all ready?'

'Yes, Chief.'

'Then I can proceed.'

He proceeded as he had done at countless congresses, at

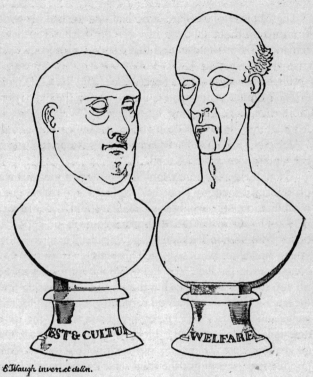

EST & CULTURE   WELFARE

E.Waugh invent et delin.

COALITION

countless spas and university cities. He concluded, as he always did: 'In the New Britain which we are building, there are no criminals. There are only the victims of inadequate social services.'

The Minister of Welfare, who had not reached his present eminence without the help of a certain sharpness in debate, remarked: 'But I understood that Plastic is from one of our own Orphanages . . .'

'Plastic is recognized as a Special Case,' said the Chief Guide.

The Minister of Rest and Culture, who in the old days had more than once done time himself, said: 'Well, Plastic, lad, from all they do say I reckon you've been uncommon smart.'

'Exactly,' said the Chief Guide. 'Miles is our first success, the vindication of the Method.'

'Of all the new prisons established in the first glorious wave of Reform, Mountjoy alone has produced a complete case of rehabilitation,' the Minister of Welfare said. 'You may or may not be aware that the Method has come in for a good deal of criticism both in Parliament and outside. There are a lot of young hot-heads who take their inspiration from our Great Neighbour in the East. You can quote the authorities to them till you're black in the face but they are always pressing for all the latest gadgets of capital and corporal punishment, for chain gangs and solitary confinement, bread and water, the cat-o'-nine-tails, the rope and the block, and all manner of new-fangled nonsense. They think we're a lot of old fogeys. Thank goodness we've still got the solid sense of the people behind us, but we're on the defensive now. We have to show results. That's why we're here this morning. To show them results. *You* are our Result.'

These were solemn words and Miles in some measure responded to the occasion. He gazed before him blankly with an expression that might seem to be awe.

'You'd best watch your step now, lad,' said Minister of Rest and Culture.

'Photographs,' said the Minister of Welfare. 'Yes, shake *my* hand. Turn towards the cameras. Try to smile.'

Bulbs flashed all over the dreary little room.

'State be with you,' said the Minister of Welfare.

'Give us a paw, lad,' said the Minister of Rest and Culture, taking Miles's hand in his turn. 'And no funny business, mind.'

Then the politicians departed.

'The Deputy-Chief will attend to all the practical matters,' said the Chief wearily. 'Go and see him now.'

Miles went.

'Well, Miles, from now on I must call you Mr Plastic,' said the Deputy-Chief. 'In less than a minute you become a Citizen. This little pile of papers is *You*. When I stamp them, Miles the Problem ceases to exist and Mr Plastic the Citizen is born. We are sending you to Satellite City, the nearest Population Centre, where you will be attached to the Ministry of Welfare as a sub-official. In view of your special training you are not being classified as a Worker. The immediate material rewards, of course, are not as great. But you are definitely in the Service. We have set your foot on the bottom rung of the non-competitive ladder.'

The Deputy Chief Guide picked up the rubber stamp and proceeded to his work of creation. Flip-thump, flip-thump, the papers were turned and stained.

'There you are, Mr Plastic,' said the Deputy-Chief handing Miles, as it were, the baby.

At last Miles spoke: 'What must I do to get back here?' he asked.

'Come, come, you're rehabilitated now, remember. It is your turn to give back to the State some of the service the

State has given you. You will report this morning to the Area Progressive. Transport has been laid on. State be with you, Mr Plastic. Be careful, that's your Certificate of Human Personality you've dropped – a *vital* document.'

2

SATELLITE CITY, one of a hundred such grand conceptions, was not yet in its teens, but already the Dome of Security showed signs of wear. This was the name of the great municipal edifice about which the city was planned. The eponymous dome had looked well enough in the architect's model, shallow certainly but amply making up in girth what it lacked in height, the daring exercise of some new trick of construction. But to the surprise of all, when the building arose and was seen from the ground, the dome blandly vanished. It was hidden for ever among the roofs and butting shoulders of the ancillary wings and was never seen again from the outside except by airmen and steeplejacks. Only the name remained. On the day of its dedication, among massed politicians and People's Choirs the great lump of building materials had shone fine as a factory in all its brilliance of glass and new concrete. Since then, during one of the rather frequent weekends of international panic, it had been camouflaged and its windows blackened. Cleaners were few and usually on strike. So the Dome of Security remained blotched and dingy, the sole permanent building of Satellite City. There were no workers' flats, no officials' garden suburb, no parks, no playgrounds yet. These were all on the drawing-boards in the surveyor's office, tattered at the edges, ringed by tea cups; their designer long since cremated and his ashes scattered among the docks and nettles. Thus the Dome of Security

EU

EXILES FRO

Canova fec. Moses delin. Waugh perfec

ΦΑΛΑCΙΑ
CLOSED
DURING
STRIKE

WELFARE

comprised, even more than had been intended, all the aspirations and amenities of the city.

The officials subsisted in perpetual twilight. Great sheets of glass, planned to 'trap' the sun, admitted few gleams from scratches in their coat of tar. At evening when the electric light came on, there was a faint glow, here and there. When, as often, the power-station was 'shedding its load' the officials stopped work early and groped their way back to their darkened huts where in the useless refrigerators their tiny rations were quietly putrefying. On working days the officials, male and female, trudged through cigarette ends round and round, up and down what had once been lift-shafts, in a silent, shabby, shadowy procession.

Among these pilgrims of the dusk, in the weeks that followed his discharge from Mountjoy, moved the exiled Miles Plastic.

He was in a key department.

Euthanasia had not been part of the original 1945 Health Service; it was a Tory measure designed to attract votes from the aged and the mortally sick. Under the Bevan–Eden Coalition the Service came into general use and won instant popularity. The Union of Teachers was pressing for its application to difficult children. Foreigners came in such numbers to take advantage of the service that immigration authorities now turned back the bearers of single tickets.

Miles recognized the importance of his appointment even before he began work. On his first evening in the hostel his fellow sub-officials gathered round to question him.

'Euthanasia? I say, you're in luck. They work you jolly hard, of course, but it's the one department that's expanding.'

'You'll get promoted before you know your way about.'

'Great State! You *must* have pull. Only the very bright boys get posted to Euthanasia.'

'I've been in Contraception for five years. It's a blind alley.'

'They say that in a year or two Euthanasia will have taken over Pensions.'

'You must be an orphan.'

'Yes, I am.'

'That accounts for it. Orphans get all the plums. I had a Full Family Life, State help me.'

It was gratifying, of course, this respect and envy. It was well to have fine prospects; but for the time being Miles's duties were humble enough.

He was junior sub-official in a staff of half a dozen. The Director was an elderly man called Dr Beamish, a man whose character had been formed in the nervous thirties, now much embittered, like many of his contemporaries, by the fulfilment of his early hopes. He had signed manifestos in his hot youth, had raised his fist in Barcelona, and had painted abstractedly for *Horizon;* he had stood beside Spender at great concourses of Youth, and written 'publicity' for the Last Viceroy. Now his reward had come to him. He held the most envied post in Satellite City and, sardonically, he was making the worst of it. Dr Beamish rejoiced in every attenuation of official difficulties.

Satellite City was said to be the worst-served Euthanasia Centre in the State. Dr Beamish's patients were kept waiting so long that often they died natural deaths before he found it convenient to poison them.

His small staff respected Dr Beamish. They were all of the official class, for it was part of the grim little game which Dr Beamish played with the higher authorities to economize extravagantly. His department, he maintained, could not, on its present allotment, afford workers. Even the furnace-man and the girl who dispatched unwanted false teeth to the Dental Redistribution Centre were sub-officials.

Sub-officials were cheap and plentiful. The Universities turned them out in thousands every year. Indeed, ever since the Incitement to Industry Act of 1955, which exempted workers from taxation – that great and popular measure of reform which had consolidated the now permanent Coalition Government – there had been a nefarious one-way traffic of expensively State-educated officials 'passing', as it was called, into the ranks of the workers.

Miles's duties required no special skill. Daily at ten the Service opened its doors to welfare-weary citizens. Miles was the man who opened them, stemmed the too eager rush, and admitted the first half dozen; then he closed the doors on the waiting multitude until a Higher Official gave the signal for the admission of another batch.

Once inside they came briefly under his charge; he set them in order, saw that they did not press ahead of their turn, and adjusted the television-set for their amusement. A Higher Official interviewed them, checked their papers, and arranged for the confiscation of their property. Miles never passed the door through which they were finally one by one conducted. A faint whiff of cyanide sometimes gave a hint of the mysteries beyond. Meanwhile he swept the waiting-room, emptied the waste-paper basket, and brewed tea – a worker's job, for which the refinements of Mountjoy proved a too rich apprenticeship.

In his hostel the same reproductions of Léger and Picasso as had haunted his childhood still stared down on him. At the cinema, to which he could afford, at the best, a weekly visit, the same films as he had seen free at Orphanage, Air Force station, and prison flickered and drawled before him. He was a child of Welfare, strictly schooled to a life of boredom, but he had known better than this. He had known the tranquil melancholy of the gardens at Mountjoy. He had known ecstasy when the Air Force Training School had whirled to the stars in a typhoon of flame. And as he moved sluggishly between Dome and hostel there rang in his ears the words of the old lag: 'You didn't give enough trouble.'

Then one day, in the least expected quarter, in his own drab department, hope appeared.

Miles later remembered every detail of that morning. It had started in the normal way; rather below normal indeed, for they were reopening after a week's enforced idleness. There had been a strike among the coal-miners and Euthanasia had been at a standstill. Now the necessary capitulations had been signed, the ovens glowed again, and the queue at the patients' entrance stretched half-way round the dome. Dr Beamish squinted at the waiting crowd through the periscope and said with some satisfaction. 'It will take months to catch up on the waiting list now. We shall have to start making a charge for the service. It's the only way to keep down the demand.'

'The Ministry will never agree to that, surely, sir?'

'Damned sentimentalists. My father and mother hanged themselves in their own back-yard with their own clothes-line. Now no one will lift a finger to help himself. There's something wrong in the system, Plastic. There are still rivers to drown in, trains – every now and then – to put your head under; gas-fires in some of the huts. The country is full of the natural resources of death, but everyone has to come to us.'

It was not often he spoke so frankly before his subordinates. He had overspent during the week's holiday, drunk too much at his hostel with other unemployed colleagues. Always after a strike the senior officials returned to work in low spirits.

'Shall I let the first batch in, sir?'

'Not for the moment,' said Dr Beamish. 'There's a priority case to see first, sent over with a pink chit from Drama. She's in the private waiting-room now. Fetch her in.'

Miles went to the room reserved for patients of importance. All one wall was of glass. Pressed to it a girl was standing, turned away from him, looking out at the glum queue below. Miles stood, the light in his eyes, conscious only of a shadow which stirred at the sound of the latch and turned, still a shadow merely but of exquisite grace, to meet him. He stood at the door, momentarily struck silent at this blind glance of beauty. Then he said: 'We're quite ready for you now, miss.'

The girl came nearer. Miles's eyes adjusted themselves to the light. The shadow took form. The full vision was all that the first glance had hinted; more than all, for every slight movement revealed perfection. One feature only broke the canon of pure beauty; a long, silken, corn-gold beard.

She said, with a deep, sweet tone, all unlike the flat conventional accent of the age: 'Let it be quite understood that I don't want anything done to me. I consented to come here. The Director of Drama and the Director of Health were so pathetic about it all that I thought it was the least I could do. I said I was quite willing to hear about your service, but I do *not* want anything *done*.'

'Better tell him inside,' said Miles.

He led her to Dr Beamish's room.

'Great State!' said Dr Beamish, with eyes for the beard alone.

'Yes,' she said. 'It is a shock, isn't it? I've got used to it by now but I can understand how people feel seeing it for the first time.'

'Is it real?'

'Pull.'

'It *is* strong. Can't they do anything about it?'

'Oh they've tried everything.'

Dr Beamish was so deeply interested that he forgot Miles's presence. 'Klugmann's Operation, I suppose?'

'Yes.'

'It does go wrong like that every now and then. They had two or three cases at Cambridge.'

'I never wanted it done. I never want anything done. It was the Head of the Ballet. He insists on all the girls being sterilized. Apparently you can never dance really well again after you've had a baby. And I did want to dance really well. Now this is what's happened.'

'Yes,' said Dr Beamish. 'Yes. They're far too slapdash. They had to put down those girls at Cambridge, too. There was no cure. Well, we'll attend to you, young lady. Have you any arrangements to make or shall I take you straight away?'

'But I don't want to be put down. I told your assistant here, I've simply consented to come at all because the Director of Drama cried so, and he's rather a darling. I've not the smallest intention of letting you kill me.'

While she spoke, Dr Beamish's geniality froze. He looked at her with hatred, not speaking. Then he picked up the pink form. 'Then this no longer applies?'

'No.'

'Then for State's sake,' said Dr Beamish, very angry, 'what are you wasting my time for? I've got more than a hundred urgent cases waiting outside and you come in here to tell me that the Director of Drama is a darling. I know the Director of Drama. We live side by side in the same ghastly hostel. He's a pest. And I'm going to write a report to the Ministry about this tomfoolery which will make him and the lunatic who thinks he can perform a Klugmann come round to be begging for extermination. And then I'll put them at the bottom of the queue. Get her out of here, Plastic, and let some sane people in.'

Miles led her into the public waiting-room. 'What an old

beast,' she said. 'What a perfect beast. I've never been spoken
to like that before even in the ballet-school. He seemed so nice
at first.'

'It's his professional feeling,' said Miles. 'He was naturally
put out at losing such an attractive patient.'

She smiled. Her beard was not so thick as quite to obscure
her delicate ovoid of cheek and chin. She might have been
peeping at him over ripe heads of barley.

Her smile started in her wide grey eyes. Her lips under her
golden moustachios were unpainted, tactile. A line of pale
down sprang below them and ran through the centre of the
chin, spreading and thickening and growing richer in colour
till it met the full flow of the whiskers, but leaving on either
side, clear and tender, two symmetrical zones, naked and
provocative. So might have smiled some carefree deacon in
the colonnaded schools of fifth-century Alexandria and struck
dumb the heresiarchs.

'I think your beard is beautiful.'

'Do you really? I can't help liking it too. I can't help liking
anything about myself, can you?'

'Yes. Oh, yes.'

'That's not natural.'

Clamour at the outer door interrupted the talk. Like gulls
round a lighthouse the impatient victims kept up an irregular
flap and slap on the panels.

'We're all ready, Plastic,' said a senior official. 'What's
going on this morning?'

What was going on? Miles could not answer. Turbulent
sea birds seemed to be dashing themselves against the light in
his own heart.

'Don't go,' he said to the girl. 'Please, I shan't be a minute.'

'Oh, I've nothing to take me away. My department all
think I'm half dead by now.'

Miles opened the door and admitted an indignant half-dozen. He directed them to their chairs, to the registry. Then he went back to the girl who had turned away slightly from the crowd and drawn a scarf peasantwise round her head, hiding her beard.

'I still don't quite like people staring,' she said.

'Our patients are far too busy with their own affairs to notice anyone else,' said Miles. 'Besides you'd have been stared at all right if you'd stayed on in ballet.'

Miles adjusted the television but few eyes in the waiting-room glanced towards it; all were fixed on the registrar's table and the doors beyond.

'Think of all them coming here,' said the bearded girl.

'We give them the best service we can,' said Miles.

'Yes, of course, I know you do. Please don't think I was finding fault. I only meant, fancy wanting to die.'

'One or two have good reasons.'

'I suppose you would say that I had. Everyone has been trying to persuade me, since my operation. The medical officials were the worst. They're afraid they may get into trouble for doing it wrong. And then the ballet people were almost as bad. They are so keen on Art that they say: "You were the best of your class. You can never dance again. How can life be worth living?" What I try to explain is that it's just because I could dance that I *know* life is worth living. That's what Art means to me. Does that sound very silly?'

'It sounds unorthodox.'

'Ah, but you're not an artist.'

'Oh, I've danced all right. Twice a week through my time at the Orphanage.'

'Therapeutic dancing?'

'That's what they called it.'

'But you see, that's quite different from Art.'

'Why?'

'Oh,' she said with a sudden full intimacy, with fondness. 'Oh what a lot you don't know.'

The dancer's name was Clara.

3

COURTSHIP was free and easy in this epoch but Miles was Clara's first lover. The strenuous exercises of her training, the austere standards of the corps-de-ballet, and her devotion to her art had kept her body and soul unencumbered.

For Miles, child of the State, Sex had been part of the curriculum at every stage of his education; first in diagrams, then in demonstrations, then in application, he had mastered all the antics of procreation. Love was a word seldom used except by politicians and by them only in moments of pure fatuity. Nothing that he had been taught prepared him for Clara.

Once in drama, always in drama. Clara now spent her days mending ballet shoes and helping neophytes on the wall bars. She had a cubicle in a Nissen hut and it was there that she and Miles spent most of their evenings. It was unlike anyone else's quarters in Satellite City.

Two little paintings hung on the walls, unlike any paintings Miles had seen before, unlike anything approved by the Ministry of Art. One represented a goddess of antiquity, naked and rosy, fondling a peacock on a bank of flowers; the other a vast, tree-fringed lake and a party in spreading silken clothes embarking in a pleasure boat under a broken arch. The gilt frames were much chipped but what remained of them was elaborately foliated.

'They're French,' said Clara. 'More than two hundred years old. My mother left them to me.'

All her possessions had come from her mother, nearly enough of them to furnish the little room – a looking glass framed in porcelain flowers, a gilt irregular clock. She and Miles drank their sad, officially compounded coffee out of brilliant, riveted cups.

'It reminds me of prison,' said Miles when he was first admitted there.

It was the highest praise he knew.

On the first evening among this delicate bric-à-brac his lips found the bare twin spaces of her chin.

'I knew it would be a mistake to let the beastly doctor poison me,' said Clara complacently.

Full summer came. Another moon waxed over these rare lovers. Once they sought coolness and secrecy among the high cow-parsley and willow-herb of the waste building sites. Clara's beard was all silvered like a patriarch's in the midnight radiance.

'On such a night as this,' said Miles, supine, gazing into the face of the moon, 'on such a night as this I burned an Air Force Station and half its occupants.'

Clara sat up and began lazily smoothing her whiskers, then more vigorously tugged the comb through the thicker, tangled growth of her head, dragging it from her forehead; re-ordered the clothing which their embraces had loosed. She was full of womanly content and ready to go home. But Miles, all male, *post coitum tristis*, was struck by a chill sense of loss. No demonstration or exercise had prepared him for this strange new experience of the sudden loneliness that follows requited love.

Walking home they talked casually and rather crossly.

'You never go to the ballet now.'

'No.'

'Won't they give you seats?'

A.CANOVA ET E.WAUGH FECERUNT

'I suppose they would.'

'Then why don't you go?'

'I don't think I should like it. I see them often rehearsing. I don't like it.'

'But you lived for it.'

'Other interests now.'

'Me?'

'Of course.'

'You love me more than the ballet?'

'I am very happy.'

'Happier than if you were dancing?'

'I can't tell, can I? You're all I've got now.'

'But if you could change?'

'I can't.'

'If?'

'There's no "if".'

'Damn.'

'Don't fret, darling. It's only the moon.'

And they parted in silence.

November came, a season of strikes; leisure for Miles, un-sought and unvalued; lonely periods when the ballet school worked on and the death house stood cold and empty.

Clara began to complain of ill health. She was growing stout.

'Just contentment,' she said at first, but the change worried her. 'Can it be that beastly operation?' she asked. 'I heard the reason they put down one of the Cambridge girls was that she kept growing fatter and fatter.'

'She weighed nineteen stone,' said Miles. 'I know because Dr Beamish mentioned it. He has strong professional objec-tions to the Klugmann operation.'

'I'm going to see the Director of Medicine. There's a new one now.'

When she returned from her appointment, Miles, still left idle by the strikers, was waiting for her among her pictures and china. She sat beside him on the bed.

'Let's have a drink,' she said.

They had taken to drinking wine together, very rarely because of the expense. The State chose and named the vintage. This month the issue was 'Progress Port'. Clara kept it in a crimson, white-cut, Bohemian flagon. The glasses were modern, unbreakable, and unsightly.

'What did the doctor say?'

'He's very sweet.'

'Well?'

'Much cleverer than the one before.'

'Did he say it was anything to do with your operation?'

'Oh, yes. Everything to do with it.'

'Can he put you right?'

'Yes, he thinks so.'

'Good.'

They drank their wine.

'That first doctor did make a mess of the operation, didn't he?'

'Such a mess. The new doctor says I'm a unique case. You see, I'm pregnant.'

'*Clara*.'

'Yes, it is a surprise, isn't it?'

'This needs thinking about,' said Miles.

He thought.

He refilled their glasses.

He said: 'It's hard luck on the poor little beast not being an Orphan. Not much opportunity for it. If he's a boy we must try and get him registered as a worker. Of course it might be a girl. Then,' brightly, 'we could make her a dancer.'

'Oh, don't mention dancing,' cried Clara, and suddenly began weeping. 'Don't speak to me of dancing.'

Her tears fell fast. No tantrum this, but deep uncontrolled inconsolable sorrow.

And next day she disappeared.

4

SANTA-CLAUS-TIDE was near. Shops were full of shoddy little dolls. Children in the schools sang old ditties about peace and goodwill. Strikers went back to work in order to qualify for their seasonal bonus. Electric bulbs were hung in the conifers and the furnaces in the Dome of Security roared again. Miles had been promoted. He now sat beside the assistant registrar and helped stamp and file the documents of the dead. It was harder work than he was used to and Miles was hungry for Clara's company. The lights were going out in the Dome and on the Goodwill Tree in the car park. He walked the half-mile of hutments to Clara's quarters. Other girls were waiting for their consorts or setting out to find them in the Recreatorium, but Clara's door was locked. A note, pinned to it, read: *Miles, Going away for a bit. C.* Angry and puzzled he returned to his hostel.

Clara, unlike himself, had uncles and cousins scattered about the country. Since her operation she had been shy of visiting them. Now, Miles supposed, she was taking cover among them. It was the manner of her flight, so unlike her gentle ways, that tortured him. For a busy week he thought of nothing else. His reproaches sang in his head as the undertone to all the activities of the day and at night he lay sleepless repeating in his mind every word spoken between them and every act of intimacy.

After a week the thought of her became spasmodic and regular. The subject bored him unendurably. He strove to

keep it out of his mind as a man might strive to control an
attack of hiccups, and as impotently. Spasmodically, mechanic-
ally, the thought of Clara returned. He timed it and found
that it came every 7½ minutes. He went to sleep thinking of
her, he woke up thinking of her. But between times he slept.
He consulted the departmental psychiatrist who told him that
he was burdened by the responsibility of parentage. But it was
not Clara the mother who haunted him, but Clara the betrayer.

Next week he thought of her every twenty minutes. The
week after that he thought of her irregularly, though often;
only when something outside himself reminded him of her.
He began to look at other girls and considered himself cured.

He looked hard at other girls as he passed them in the dim
corridors of the Dome and they looked boldly back at him.
Then one of them stopped him and said: 'I've seen you before
with Clara', and at the mention of her name all interest in the
other girl ceased in pain. 'I went to visit her yesterday.'

'Where?'

'In hospital, of course. Didn't you know?'

'What's the matter with her?'

'She won't say. Nor will anyone else at the hospital. She's
top secret. If you ask me she's been in an accident and there's
some politician involved. I can't think of any other reason for
all the fuss. She's covered in bandages and gay as a lark.'

Next day, 25 December, was Santa Claus Day; no holiday
in the department of Euthanasia, which was an essential service.
At dusk Miles walked to the hospital, one of the unfinished
edifices, all concrete and steel and glass in front and a jumble
of huts behind. The hall porter was engrossed in the television,
which was performing an old obscure folk play which past
generations had performed on Santa Claus Day, and was now
revived and revised as a matter of historical interest.

It was of professional interest to the porter for it dealt with

TIDINGS OF COMFORT AND JOY

maternity services before the days of Welfare. He gave the number of Clara's room without glancing up from the strange spectacle of an ox and an ass, an old man with a lantern, and a young mother. 'People here are always complaining,' he said. 'They ought to realize what things were like before Progress.'

The corridors were loud with relayed music. Miles found the hut he sought. It was marked 'Experimental Surgery. Health Officers only.' He found the cubicle. He found Clara sleeping, the sheet pulled up to her eyes, her hair loose on the pillow. She had brought some of her property with her. An old shawl lay across the bed-table. A painted fan stood against the television set. She awoke, her eyes full of frank welcome and pulled the sheet higher, speaking through it.

'Darling, you shouldn't have come. I was keeping it for a surprise.'

Miles sat by the bed and thought of nothing to say except: 'How are you?'

'Wonderful. They've taken the bandages off today. They won't let me have a looking glass yet but they say everything has been a tremendous success. I'm something very special, Miles – a new chapter in surgical progress.'

'But what has happened to you. Is it something to do with the baby?'

'Oh no. At least, it was. That was the first operation. But that's all over now.'

'You mean our child?'

'Yes, that had to go. I should never have been able to dance afterwards. I told you all about it. That was why I had the Klugmann operation, don't you remember?'

'But you gave up dancing.'

'That's where they've been so clever. Didn't I tell you about the sweet, clever new medical director? He's cured all that.'

EXPERIMENTAL SURGERY

'Your dear beard.'

'Quite gone. An operation the new director invented himself. It's going to be named after him or even perhaps after me. He's so unselfish he wants to call it the Clara Operation. He's taken off all the skin and put on a wonderful new substance, a sort of synthetic rubber that takes grease-paint perfectly. He says the colour isn't perfect, but that it will never show on the stage. Look, feel it.'

She sat up in bed, joyful and proud.

Her eyes and brow were all that was left of the loved face.

Below it something quite inhuman, a tight, slippery mask, salmon pink.

Miles stared. In the television screen by the bed further characters had appeared – Food Production Workers. They seemed to declare a sudden strike, left their sheep, and ran off at the bidding of some kind of shop-steward in fantastic dress. The machine by the bedside broke into song, an old, forgotten ditty: 'O tidings of comfort and joy, comfort and joy, O tidings of comfort and joy.'

Miles retched unobtrusively. The ghastly face regarded him with fondness and pride. At length the right words came to him; the trite, the traditional sentence uttered by countless lips of generations of baffled and impassioned Englishmen: 'I think I shall go for a short walk.'

But first he walked only as far as his hostel. There he lay down until the moon moved to his window and fell across his sleepless face. Then he set out, walking far into the fields, out of sight of the Dome of Security, for two hours until the moon was near setting.

He had travelled at random but now the white rays fell on a signpost and he read: 'Mountjoy ¾.' He strode on with only the stars to light his way till he came to the Castle gates.

They stood open as always, gracious symbol of the new penology. He followed the drive. The whole lightless face of the old house stared at him silently, without rebuke. He knew now what was needed. He carried in his pocket a cigarette lighter which often worked. It worked for him now.

No need for oil here. The dry old silk of the drawing-room curtains lit like paper. Paint and panelling, plaster and tapestry and gilding bowed to the embrace of the leaping flames. He stepped outside. Soon it was too hot on the terrace and he retreated further, to the marble temple at the end of the long walk. The murderers were leaping from the first-storey windows but the sexual offenders, trapped above, set up a wail of terror. He heard the chandeliers fall and saw the boiling lead cascading from the roof. This was something altogether finer than the strangulation of a few peacocks. He watched exultant as minute by minute the scene disclosed fresh wonders. Great timbers crashed within; outside the lily-pond hissed with falling brands; a vast ceiling of smoke shut out the stars and under it tongues of flame floated away into the tree tops.

Two hours later when the first engine arrived, the force of the fiery storm was already spent. Miles rose from his marble throne and began the long walk home. But he was no longer at all fatigued. He strode out cheerfully with his shadow, cast by the dying blaze, stretching before him along the lane.

On the main road a motorist stopped him and asked: 'What's that over there? A house on fire?'

'It was,' said Miles. 'It's almost out now.'

'Looks like a big place. Only Government property, I suppose?'

'That's all,' said Miles.

'Well hop in if you want a lift.'

'Thanks,' said Miles. 'I'm walking for pleasure.'

MILES rose after two hours in bed. The hostel was alive with all the normal activity of morning. The wireless was playing; the sub-officials were coughing over their wash-basins; the reek of State sausages frying in State grease filled the asbestos cubicle. He was slightly stiff after his long walk and slightly footsore, but his mind was as calm and empty as the sleep from which he had awoken. The scorched-earth policy had succeeded. He had made a desert in his imagination which he might call peace. Once before, he had burned his childhood. Now his brief adult life lay in ashes; the enchantments that surrounded Clara were one with the splendours of Mountjoy; her great golden beard, one with the tongues of flame that had leaped and expired among the stars; her fans and pictures and scraps of old embroidery, one with the gilded cornices and silk hangings, black, cold, and sodden. He ate his sausage with keen appetite and went to work.

All was quiet too at the Department of Euthanasia.

The first announcement of the Mountjoy disaster had been on the early news. Its proximity to Satellite City gave it a special poignancy there.

'It is a significant phenomenon,' said Dr Beamish, 'that any bad news has an immediate effect on our service. You see it whenever there is an international crisis. Sometimes I think people only come to us when they have nothing to talk about. Have you looked at our queue today?'

Miles turned to the periscope. Only one man waited outside, old Parsnip, a poet of the thirties who came daily but was usually jostled to the back of the crowd. He was a comic character in the department, this veteran poet. Twice in Miles's short term he had succeeded in gaining admission but on both occasions had suddenly taken fright and bolted.

'It's a lucky day for Parsnip,' said Miles.

'Yes. He deserves some luck. I knew him well once, him and his friend Pimpernell. *New Writing*, the Left Book Club, they were all the rage. Pimpernell was one of my first patients. Hand Parsnip in and we'll finish him off.'

So old Parsnip was summoned and that day his nerve stood firm. He passed fairly calmly through the gas chamber on his way to rejoin Pimpernell.

'We might as well knock off for the day,' said Dr Beamish. 'We shall be busy again soon when the excitement dies down.'

But the politicians determined to keep the excitement up. All the normal features of television were interrupted and curtailed to give place to Mountjoy. Survivors appeared on the screen, among them Soapy, who described how long practice as a cat burglar had enabled him to escape. Mr Sweat, he remarked with respect, had got clear away. The ruins were surveyed by the apparatus. A sexual maniac with broken legs gave audience from his hospital bed. The Minister of Welfare, it was announced, would make a special appearance that evening to comment on the disaster.

Miles dozed intermittently beside the hostel set and at dusk rose, still calm and free; so purged of emotion that he made his way once more to the hospital and called on Clara.

She had spent the afternoon with looking-glass and make-up box. The new substance of her face fulfilled all the surgeon's promises. It took paint to perfection. Clara had given herself a full mask as though for the lights of the stage; an even

PARSNIP AD PORTUS

creamy white with sudden high spots of crimson on the cheek bones, huge hard crimson lips, eye brows extended and turned up catwise, the eyes shaded all round with ultramarine and dotted at the corners with crimson.

'You're the first to see me,' she said. 'I was half-afraid you wouldn't come. You seemed cross yesterday.'

'I wanted to see the television,' said Miles. 'It's so crowded at the hostel.'

'So dull today. Nothing except this prison that has been burned down.'

'I was there myself. Don't you remember? I often talked of it.'

'Did you, Miles? Perhaps so. I've such a bad memory for things that don't concern me. Do you really want to hear the Minister? It would be much cosier to talk.'

'It's him I've come for.'

And presently the Minister appeared, open-necked as always but without his usual smile; grave to the verge of tears. He spoke for twenty minutes. '. . . The great experiment must go on . . . the martyrs of maladjustment shall not have died in vain . . . A greater, new Mountjoy shall rise from the ashes of the old . . .' Eventually tears came – real tears for he held an invisible onion – and trickled down his cheeks. So the speech ended.

'That's all I came for,' said Miles, and left Clara to her cocoa-butter and face-towel.

Next day all the organs of public information were still piping the theme of Mountjoy. Two or three patients, already bored with the entertainment, presented themselves for extermination and were happily dispatched. Then a message came from the Regional Director, official-in-chief of Satellite City. He required the immediate presence of Miles in his office.

'I have a move order for you, Mr Plastic. You are to report to the Ministers of Welfare and Rest and Culture. You will be issued with a Grade A hat, umbrella, and brief case for the journey. My congratulations.'

Equipped with these insignia of sudden, dizzy promotion, Miles travelled to the capital leaving behind a domeful of sub-officials chattering with envy.

At the terminus an official met him. Together in an official car they drove to Whitehall.

'Let me carry your brief-case, Mr Plastic.'

'There's nothing in it.'

Miles's escort laughed obsequiously at this risqué joke.

At the Ministry the lifts were in working order. It was a new and alarming experience to enter the little cage and rise to the top of the great building.

'Do they always work here?'

'Not *always*, but very very often.'

Miles realized that he was indeed at the heart of things.

'Wait here. I will call you when the Ministers are ready.'

Miles looked from the waiting-room window at the slow streams of traffic. Just below him stood a strange, purposeless obstruction of stone. A very old man, walking by, removed his hat to it as though saluting an acquaintance. Why? Miles wondered. Then he was summoned to the politicians.

They were alone in their office save for a gruesome young woman. The Minister of Rest and Culture said: 'Ease your feet, lad' and indicated a large leatherette armchair.

'Not such a happy occasion, alas, as our last meeting,' said the Minister of Welfare.

'Oh, I don't know,' said Miles. He was enjoying the outing.

'The tragedy at Mountjoy Castle was a grievous loss to the cause of penology.'

'But the great work of Rehabilitation will continue,' said the gruesome young woman.

'A greater Mountjoy will arise from the ashes,' said the Minister.

'Those noble criminal lives have not been lost in vain.'

'Their memory will inspire us.'

'Yes,' said Miles. 'I heard the broadcast.'

'Exactly,' said the Minister. 'Precisely. Then you appreciate, perhaps, what a change the occurrence makes in your own position. From being, as we hoped, the first of a continuous series of successes, you are our only one. It would not be too much to say that the whole future of penology is in your hands. The destruction of Mountjoy Castle by itself was merely a setback. A sad one, of course, but something which might be described as the growing pains of a great movement. But there is a darker side. I told you, I think, that our great experiment had been made only against considerable opposition. Now – I speak confidentially – that opposition has become vocal and unscrupulous. There is, in fact, a whispering campaign that the fire was no accident but the act of one of the very men whom we were seeking to serve. That campaign must be scotched.'

'They can't do us down as easy as they think,' said the Minister of Rest and Culture. 'Us old dogs know a trick or two.'

'Exactly. Counter-propaganda. You are our Exhibit A. The irrefutable evidence of the triumph of our system. We are going to send you up and down the country to lecture. My colleagues have already written your speech. You will be accompanied by Miss Flower here, who will show and explain the model of the new Mountjoy. Perhaps you will care to see it yourself. Miss Flower, the model please.'

All the time they had been speaking Miles had been aware of a bulky sheeted object on a table in the window. Miss Flower now unveiled it. Miles gazed in awe.

The object displayed was a familiar, standard packing-case, set on end.

'A rush-job,' said the Minister of Welfare. 'You will be provided with something more elaborate for your tour.'

Miles gazed at the box.

It fitted. It fell into place precisely in the void of his mind, satisfying all the needs for which his education had prepared him. The conditioned personality recognized its proper preordained environment. All else was insubstantial; the gardens of Mountjoy, Clara's cracked Crown Derby and her enveloping beard were trophies of a fading dream.

The Modern Man was home.

'There is one further point,' continued the Minister of Welfare. 'A domestic one but not as irrelevant as it may seem. Have you by any chance formed an attachment in Satellite City? Your dossier suggests that you have.'

'Any woman trouble?' explained the Minister of Rest and Culture.

'Oh, yes,' said Miles. 'Great trouble. But that is over.'

'You see, perfect rehabilitation, complete citizenship should include marriage.'

'It has not,' said Miles.

'That should be rectified.'

'Folks like a bloke to be spliced,' said the Minister of Rest and Culture. 'With a couple of kids.'

'There is hardly time for *them*,' said the Minister of Welfare. 'But we think that psychologically you will have more appeal if you have a wife by your side. Miss Flower here has every qualification.'

'Looks are only skin deep, lad,' said the Minister of Rest and Culture.

'So if you have no preferable alternative to offer . . .?'

'None,' said Miles.

'Spoken like an Orphan. I see a splendid career ahead of the pair of you.'

'When can we get divorced?'

'Come, come, Plastic. You mustn't look too far ahead. First things first. You have already obtained the necessary leave from your Director, Miss Flower?'

'Yes, Minister.'

'Then off you both go. And State be with you.'

In perfect peace of heart Miles followed Miss Flower to the Registrar's office.

Then the mood veered.

Miles felt ill at ease during the ceremony and fidgeted with something small and hard which he found in his pocket. It proved to be his cigarette-lighter, a most uncertain apparatus. He pressed the catch and instantly, surprisingly, there burst out a tiny flame – gemlike, hymeneal, auspicious.